Dedication

My motivation, my inspiration, my mother.

Acknowledgements

I also give thanks to my family for their love, support and encouragement, especially to you Ebony, for your patience and for being you.

Amari, thanks for your technical support.

Welcome by Roslyn Blaize

My name is Rose Blaize and I was born in Forest Gate, East London. We were raised by beautiful parents who loved us, my siblings and I. My parents were traditional West Indians who savoured their values, exercising good manners, order in the home, worked hard and maintained strong relations with their extended families with whom we are closely bonded. Those values of family unity live on in our family, together we are united and support one another in times of sorrow and gladness.

I attended a comprehensive inner-city school, where we dreaded the cane, respected our elders and had double portions of 'Jam roly poly' for lunch. You greeted your neighbour and had a strong sense of community. We, my generation understood the value of education and respect towards one another. A gift given to us by or parents from a different cultural strain.

I grew up in a melting pot of different racial and cultural expression. I was to some extent by default of my experience a part of the rich tapestry of my environment, being urban London. This fashioned my interaction and the way in which I related to others. I have always had a caring nature person and qualified as a social worker in the social welfare in 1996. I have had the privilege of working with many different professionals and young people of all ages, so much so, that I was able to combine those experiences; those similarities, yet unique scenarios, in order to give back by way of virtues, such as kindness, attentiveness, positive regard and respectfulness which was gratefully received by those who were experiencing vulnerability and hardship. Observing these external struggles left me in a state of gratitude for all that I possessed and felt the need to be available, to enable, to empower others. My mother died nearly 3 years ago and I was devastated but I understood that I live on as an extension of her and had to extend and grow. I know she's proud of me, as is my father.

So, I completed, **'Truthingdom'** the series. I will go on to write more books that are meaningful, that talk of purpose and significance.

Enjoy, Enjoy!

Truthingdom
The Conception

1.

The silence was deafening; the air stood still. She listened intently, drawing warm air erratically through the quilt pressing below her moistened nose. Her eyes piercing into the darkness like an eagle targeting her prey at night. She could hear steady footsteps softly approaching her room door: they stopped: she listened. Adrenaline was now pumping fiercely above her nostrils. Her eye sockets were bulging, strained with fear, dread and panic. Her fingers ached as she gripped the quilt tightly, hugging it against her cheeks.

The door slowly opened. She was able to distinguish a huge figure moving towards her, engulfing the space around it. She could feel paralysis slowly creeping from her ankles up towards her shins. Consumed with fear and feelings of entrapment and despair, she closed her eyes; warm tears seeped across her face.

She was now conscious of shallow, irregular breathing which quickened as the silhouette drew closer. She could now feel sharp short breaths close to her lips, his hands stroking her thighs then quickly travelling up towards her bosom. In repulsion, she turned her head away trying to transport herself to another time and place. Her pillow was now soaked with tears, and she was aware that she was pressing against the wall adjacent to her bed.

Tia jerked violently, arching her back while thrusting her head unto its crown, her chin pointed up towards the ceiling; her body doused in sweat. She threw her body forward; squinting as the sunlight pierced her eyes.

She looked around and sighed anxiously, thumping her clenched fists into her bed covers. She had been dreaming about the past again, circumstances that she had been desperately trying to forget; to obliterate completely.

"You hungry T?" Archie called from the stove where he was preparing scrambled eggs, coated in melted butter, which mingled with the aroma of fried bacon rashers.

Tia's studio flat was part of a loft conversion at the top of a three storey townhouse in Pimlico. She shared the studio flat with another student called Archie, who was one of Tia's links, back in the day.

"Nah," Tia replied, "I can't face food this early in the morning." She drew on the cigarette she had just lit. Her cheekbones sunk into her face, creating hollows as she pulled smoke deep into her windpipe. She felt the nicotine rush as the smoke hit the back of her throat.

She then turned her attention to new beginnings, as today was her first day at the most prestigious and illustrious Fashion Arts college in London. She had imagined what it might be like, who would be there and whether she would like it. She sprang up from the couch, which doubled up as a sofa bed and headed for the window.

The magnolia painted walls of the studio flat displayed graduated shades of brown as it crept towards the ceiling, ending in crusted orange wallpaper dog ends which peeled away from the corners at the edges. The carpet, now dull crimson, was once a vibrant cherry red.

Tia looked out past the paint stripped windowsill which still had white paint embedded in the impressions of the grain. She watched as people were rushing by, preoccupied with their thoughts and going about their daily business. They had no time to offer her encouragement, to acknowledge the importance of this, her very first day at college. This would be her chance to take control of her life and to make positive choices which she hoped would promote her own potential beyond her wildest dreams.

She was suddenly overwhelmed with thoughts of wanting to achieve, to succeed, to win.

Tia had been raised in care from the age of ten. Being separated from her mother and siblings was painful. She craved love and affection; however, her mother was preoccupied, pleasing the men in her life. Tia thought that her mother was desperately seeking security through marriage: later she realised it to be the need for self- love and acceptance.

Other than being deprived of her mother's attention, Tia was also resentful that her mother ignored the fact that Tia was black, a mixed-race child. As a child, Tia constantly tried to reaffirm who she was. Her mother's inadvertent (or was it blatant) disregard of this cast doubt on her own self-approval; her self-acceptance. The sad truth is Tia felt these feelings; however, she could not decipher how to process them. She had become the master of shutting off her emotions; not to feel. She was unable to analyse or review the impact of her feelings.

She developed a somewhat displaced view of who she was and where she fitted in. She pandered to her mother's impressions of who she was racially because she needed to fit in, to try to make sense of who she was as she grew older.

"Who am I?" She whispered to herself. Feelings of fear and abandonment gripped her soul. She felt empty. Staring out of the window, she shut her eyes and took a deep breath.

Tia's siblings reflected one another and found confirmation of themselves in each other. They were white and had straight hair.

As a child, Tia began to realise that she was different and often felt hurt and alone in a room full of people, her people, her own family. She convinced herself this was how it was, discounting her instinctive feelings for what she now saw as a lie.

Tia grew up on a council estate where older people despised each other's differences and prejudged the values of one another, exalting their own principles and ideals in place of unified expression.

Tia's voice rose above; she was an extrovert. A trait she had developed to be noticed, to be counted amongst the rest; yet unsure about why she needed to try so hard to fit in, to belong. She would shy from common sense, which hit closer to the truth when trying to make sense of her life. As a young adult, she now wanted to comprehend how past issues had impacted on her life.

Staring out of the window Tia began to smile, feeling triumphant and victorious, having been granted a scholarship to attend one of the top Fashion Schools in London. She was filled with excitement and expectation looking forward to the day ahead.

Tia then uttered, "I'm nervous and excited at the same time; I need to do this." She felt defeated; already needing to convince herself of the need to finish what she had started.

"You'll be OK; just stay focused," Archie replied. Tia was somehow reassured by his calm and affirmed response.

2.

The main lecture hall was filled with the smell of new books and a chorus of voices murmuring below the raised voice of someone struggling to converse on his mobile phone. Tia looked around, sizing up the girls and the boys. She paid particular attention to the fashion trends represented in the lecture hall, as fashion was her passion.

Tia's eyes were drawn to an Asian girl across the classroom who was dressed in a beautifully woven salwar kameez. Her attire was a rich tapestry of deep violet and luscious pink with violet embroidered lace on the edging. She wore quaint, intricately designed gemstones, set in dangling gold earrings, with an amethyst singlet stone hanging from a thin gold chain around her eloquent elongated neck.

Aarti moved, catching a glance of Tia staring back at her. Tia then looked away, focusing her attention on a group of guys at the front of the class who had been recently acquainted. She could tell this from their awkward dialogue and nervous chatter.

Tia now felt isolated and indifferent, observing what she surmised as middle-class buffoons coming from privileged homes. She deduced this by their accents and proper use of language. Tia felt incongruent up against the likes of them, coming from the *'Ends'*.

The *'Ends'* are described as an urban locality; a community which is identified by postcodes within inner cities. Tia grew up in a place where unemployment and crime were significantly higher than in other parts of the country, and its inhabitants were socially dubbed as the *'underclass'*.

"Good morning students." Tia snapped out of her daydream and focused solely on the teacher who stood just inside the doorway of the classroom. He wore a figure-hugging shirt, which Tia described as *'fluffy'* and waved his hand loosely in the air while ushering students to take their seats. He was tall, slender and wearing high-waisted black trousers. His demeanour was somewhat peculiar. Looking down his nose at everyone, avoiding eye contact and checking his fingernails intermittently before folding them across his crossed legs.

Mr Souche explained that he had been lecturing at the college for a number of years. His lack of enthusiasm was reflected in his verbal presentation, which was somewhat dull and laboured. Observing this, Tia had mixed feelings of disappointment and excitement as this was the first lesson of the day. Nevertheless, she decided to remain optimistic, extracting the positive aspects of the morning session.

The second period after lunch was trying for Tia and she was becoming bored with the monotony of it all. Although she was glad to be there, the constraints of sitting in confined spaces for extended periods of time was frustrating.

Tia reflected back to the days when she attended the pupil referral unit and had fag breaks and a part-time timetable. She found herself in a dilemma: wanting to stay; wanting to leave. Her mind played havoc with her better reason, and she quickly excused herself from the classroom.

In the ladies' toilets, Tia deeply exhaled as she blew out the mellow blend of a roll-up she had savoured from the lunch period. Turning from side to side, she cupped her hands on her sternum while looking at herself up and down, *"Apple-shaped rump and midriff with the curves..."* she started to sing as she gyrated her hips with slow, calculated precision. As her eyes met her reflection, she began to laugh, "Boy, don't I look fly," as she began to walk away and headed for the exit.

Later that afternoon Tia arrived early for her last lecture, and she was determined to remain optimistic about her choice to study fashion design, in fact, to study at all.

On entering the classroom, she observed Aarti's solitary figure poised at the far end of the room. She muttered, "Hi," and sat on the opposite side of the room. Aarti acknowledged her greeting with a slight bow of the head. Aarti then coyly turned to face Tia and commented on the dismal weather outside. Tia quickly responded, relieved that the awkward silence had been broken. The conversation then flourished. Tia spoke about her love for fashion design and Aarti about her desire to be an editor of a famous fashion magazine.

3.

Aarti was born in Alwar, west of Jaipur. She was raised by her grandparents until the age of four. Her grandparents lived in a farming district and were themselves farmers who tilled the arduous desert soil all their lives. They placed all their hopes and aspirations in their son's future and Krishna's blessings on his life. They worked hard and invested all they had in their son's destiny.

From a young age, Vishnu had developed wisdom beyond his years. He was a learned and gentle natured man who became a social activist and political figure in his community, advocating for those who were poor and downtrodden.

Aarti's father, Vishnu, later observed those inherent traits in his daughter, stimulated and nurtured by a passionate love for her people and the need to speak out against human rights injustices, especially against the oppression of tribal women and children in the remote areas of Rajasthan.

As a teenager, Aarti had gone to live in central Jaipur with her parents in the suburban district of Hasanpura, where her father worked at the National engineering industries company where he committed a lot of his time and energies to developing innovative designs of industrial machinery; his vision was to develop industry and promote economic wealth in more impoverished communities.

Aarti's mother devoted her life to nurturing her family and devotional prayer. Aarti's mother, Aditi, had long since found resolution and acceptance following years of continual prayers and offerings for a male child and given thanks for her only child, Aarti.

Truthingdom

Aarti attended a distinguished pre-school in Durgapura and later attended one of the oldest and most prestigious schools for girls in the wider region of Jaipur. This institution was historically renowned for dispelling the social stigma of the purdah, the ancient practice of concealing and segregating women from men. These women's rights were more often suppressed.

The school believed in advocating for the emancipation of women by instilling the values of education and celebrating the rites of passage leading from dependence to independence upon graduation.

Aarti was a silently confident person who understood her thoughts and feelings and instinctively observed the hierarchical stronghold within her cultural setting. Aarti harboured her views about the oppression of women in her extended family and community, as it was common practice for women to be instructed or guided by males in making important decisions which usually had a profound effect on their lives.

She was deeply religious and found escapism through prayer to voice her true feelings, to vent her frustration, explore her dreams and map out her future. In her mind, her karma was set. She pursued her dream to travel to a prominent capital city to fulfil her desire to work within the fashion industry. These ambitions were driven; having observed the tailored, mundane lifestyle her mother led.

Aarti was haunted by childhood memories of what she deemed a violation of the innocent which had been committed in the remote village where she grew up. Her younger cousin had been promised for marriage at the age of seven. On her 10th birthday, Aarti's cousin had been wed.

Aarti recalled the merriment of music and an array of colours. After the marriage ceremony, her cousin had gone to live with her husband who was nearly 15 years older than her. Aarti's father later explained that her uncle needed the dowry to pay his debts. 18 months later her cousin gave birth to a baby boy. Aarti's father revealed that there was an uproar following the birth of the baby as her cousin's husband had promised to wait until she had at least reached the age of sixteen, before having intercourse with her.

As a teenager, Aarti recalled being alarmed by these all too common events and became quietly fearful of the powers which wielded their authority so freely.

Poverty more often being the ruler of destiny and master of fate in her homeland, she was thankful for the divine favour which had been bestowed upon her parents and the blessings showered on their lives.

Through learnt experiences of oppression by virtue of her sex, Aarti acquired the social graces and wisdom to navigate her way through contested and acrimonious domestic issues presented within families in her own community. As a social advocate, she was able to negotiate and advocate for the poor and destitute in her family's village.

As a young woman, Aarti was determined to be self-sustaining, able to decide her own destiny, to take pride in her achievements and navigate life's challenges.

Schooling in England was another target fulfilled. She never took for granted the opportunity to further her education. Education unlocked doors, awarded her the respect of others and the confidence to articulate her message of equality between the sexes.

Aarti felt nervous excitement being in one of the most prestigious capitals of the world, yet anxious at not having the security of home. She missed her parents and the familiar smells of barbecued corn, incense and the sounds of the crickets, especially at night.

London's wind-wrapped skyscrapers were a stark difference from the mellow warm surroundings of Jaipur. She was curious about the mixed diversity of cultures and cosmopolitan communities in urban London. She smiled and breathed a sigh of relief, she had it all to discover and felt triumphant as she began sprinting on the spot more vigorously. She then collapsed onto her bed and drifted off to sleep.

4.

Entering the classroom, the following morning, Aarti greeted Tia, who was talking to a tall, chiselled faced man. Aarti observed his flirtatious manner and sat quietly adjacent to them. He was articulate and assertive in his dialogue. She was alerted by his confident demeanour and charisma. She wondered if he characterised the English gent.

Tia hurriedly explained that his name was Xavier and that he lived in Richmond with his parents and wanted to be an editor of a successful newspaper.

Aarti thought he was handsome and wondered about his lifestyle and his family. Tia began speaking about dinner last night. Her flatmate Archie had cooked chilli con carne and then had thrown up all over the floor, having drunk too much beer.

Tia noted that Aarti was distracted in thought and focused her attentions on the lecturer as she entered the room.

Tia was inquisitive to know more about Aarti and her life in India. Aarti later spoke to Tia about Lord Ganesh, Ramayana and Garuda; Hindu deities she had placed in her shrine. She described the communion, spiritual strength and wholeness of having a relationship with her supreme God, Brahman, and her devotion to worshipping him.

Tia raised her eyebrows and asked Aarti, "Have you always been religious?"

Aarti looked puzzled and said, "What do you mean? Do you not believe in god?"

Tia stuttered, "Well, I attended church a few times when I was younger." Aarti appeared to be bewildered by her response. Tia then felt the need to compensate, insisting that God was in each and every one of us spiritual beings and that religion was designed to control us. Archie often spoke to Tia about his ideal; that Christianity, Islam and Judaism derived from one knowledge. Archie's view of religion was often widely debated amongst friends.

Aarti was dumbfounded by Tia's casual outlook on religion and chose not to respond. Tia appeared defiant, maintaining eye contact. Aarti then asked Tia about her family. Tia smirked, slumping back in her chair. She then quickly composed herself and stated that her mother lived in East London with her younger sister, Kary. Tia's brother seldom visited the family. He lived in Essex with his girlfriend. Tia then turned her attention to other students in the lecture hall to deter further probing.

Tia preferred not to talk about her family as this invoked sad memories. She loved them, but reminiscing made her weak and angry. Tia focused on Aarti once again, "What about your future plans?"

Aarti spoke about running her own fashion magazine and her childhood fantasy; dressing up and pretending to be a Bollywood film star. Tia laughed as Aarti motioned her arms back and forth miming an Indian dance. Tia liked Aarti's immaculate dress sense; the intricate designs, styles and colours of her salwar kameez outfits and matching accessories. Tia often complimented Aarti.

Tia then talked about her ambition to become a fashion arts designer for a prestigious fashion house and travelling the world.

They were relaxed now and stimulated by discussions about their individual career pathways; destined to succeed.

Later that evening Aarti cried silently to herself. The frustration and sense of guilt was overwhelming. She gripped the airmail letter in her hands and stared for what seemed like hours outside her bedroom window. She was torn between her loyalty to her parents and her desire to be autonomous.

Aarti's parents planned to introduce her to an esteemed gentleman within the local community who had proposed marriage. Aarti had met him on several occasions, in wider social functions amongst family and friends and thought he was pleasant.

Aarti agreed with arranged marriages in principle. When she considered that the man and his family were vetted for suitability, this in itself gave the bride a sense of security. However, she thought being bound by matrimony in one's youth and state of immaturity, one's hopes were further stifled by tradition and customs which did not allow for the benefits of maturity and informed choice. Her bloated stomach ached; she felt a heaving sensation and ran to the toilet. She then sat motionless on her bed, cuddling her belly, harbouring a sense of despair.

5.

Xavier's beer was cold and refreshing. He sighed as the cool elixir's sensation travelled through his upper torso. The sun's ray penetrated his closed eyelids as he lay stretched out on the sun lounger on the patio. "Would you like another beer?" his mother called out.

"No thanks," he replied disconcertedly, "I have not finished this one yet." His father appeared quietly agitated and prodded at the sirloin steak sizzling on the barbecue. Xavier smiled, noting his father's annoyance. Xavier's mother was a psychotherapist who now spent her time maintaining her vegetable garden and talking to spirits. His father was a practising solicitor based in the City of London, near Leadenhall Street.

"Are you joining us in the highlands this year Xavier?" her speech slightly slurred. It was one o'clock in the afternoon in her hand her fourth glass of Chardonnay.

"I am not sure; I had plans to visit friends in Europe this autumn." His mother looked disappointed. Xavier noted his father withdrawing into the house, whispering intently on his phone whilst looking over his shoulder to see if the others had noticed. The phone rang, and his mother sprung to life, straightening her back as if sitting to attention and began addressing the caller on the phone.

Xavier loved his mother but despised her for shielding herself from the wrath of his father by diving into a bottle, leaving him exposed to the heartless, calculated ambition which drove his father to succeed. Success being a place where his father felt secure and self- fulfilled. Xavier understood his father well; facets of whom were exhibited in his own mannerisms.

Xavier had long since been divorced from his feelings, yet on occasion overwhelmed with uncontrollable feelings of compassion and empathy, not knowing how to interpret or express the sensations he felt.

The heat was now intense, burning his shoulders and the side of his face. Xavier strolled into the shaded conservatory. He scented the musty earth from the seedling pots lined up along the windowsill; mingled with the bouquet of honeysuckle and jasmine. He observed the creeping ivy, travelling toward the southern sun, pinned up above the Georgian style windows.

Reminiscing, Xavier was again filled with sadness and loss. Those feelings evoked painful memories of crying silently to himself whilst lying in bed, self- soothing in his dormitory in the dead of night. He had learnt no one was coming to rescue him from his misery, finding solace only in the comradeship of the boys in Tempest house, of which he had been a part. He had missed his parents, even though they had taught him, by design of their lifestyles and preoccupation, not to rely on them but to nurture his intuitive talents and desires. Xavier had also hosted and emulated aspects of their own ultra- egos. He was unconvinced they truly understood what they had cultivated in the darker side of his nature.

Xavier pandered to his mother's whims. He was the perfect gentleman, having mastered etiquette long since rehearsed in the backdrop of his privileged existence.

Xavier's thoughts turned to Tia. He had reserved thoughts about Tia and was curious about the social environment emerging at the fashion arts college. Xavier thought Tia's overt flirtatious nature to be vulgar and unappealing, yet he was flattered by her gravitation to his seeming charm and personality.

Xavier was a proud man, perpetually nourishing his zest for power and control, compensating for where his mother let him down, as well as the need to compete; measuring up to his father's ideals of strength and authority.

Xavier recalled the first week of college. He remembered the sounds and smells which drifted up into the open auditorium's expansive roof space and blacked out walls. He sensed the excitement buzzing as young pre-graduates greeted one another, filled with curiosity about the unfolding day's events. He imagined owning his own publishing house or being the editor of a prime-time magazine. He wanted popularity and fame, money and power. These things he valued above all else.

6.

It was 9:15 am, and Xavier was sitting slightly distracted by his own thoughts whilst observing the fluid dynamics in the newly formed seminar group. The topic presented: Image v Reality TV.

Mr Souche asked the group to consider whether reality TV personalities and lifestyles dictate *'Image'* or whether they both actually represent different things, and how the concept of image influences or affects our society.

Tyresse, another student who had been placed in the same study group as Xavier, was energetic and witty, handsome and lean. His tender, chocolate- brown skin glowed against his defined features; an asset which drew the opposite sex like a magnet.

Tyresse began by explaining that imagery is observed: perceived according to one's interpretation. Reality TV abets sensationalism, fuelled by profit which tends to promote false hope, and exhibits privileged lifestyles our communities fantasise about. Tyresse appeared to be on a flow, expressing his views about the lack of responsibility demonstrated by media moguls who, in his opinion, take advantage of the consumer who was hungry for escapism and a romanticised existence against the backdrop of what the consumer may describe as their mundane lives.

"Excuse me!" Tyresse exclaimed. Xavier snapped out of a daydream and faced Tyresse, his mouth slightly ajar with an apologetic look on his face. Tyresse asked again, "What's your view?" Xavier asked Tyresse to elaborate on the question, buying time to recoup in order to gain a fuller understanding of what Tyresse had been passionate about.

Xavier now sighed under his breath and sat back in his chair, looking solemn, staring at Tyresse who was once again becoming animated and hijacking the conversation to express another relative point to the argument.

"Are we boring you?" Tracey asked Xavier in a brash and direct tone.

"No, no," Xavier immediately shot upright in his chair, "I was listening."

"Yea right," Tracey responded, sounding unconvinced. Folding her arms and crossing one knee over the other, Tracey watched him from the side of her eye.

Xavier avoided her penetrating gaze. "I think individuals are prompted and or motivated by their emotional responses fashioned in their youth. They are manipulated according to their weaknesses and desires."

"An expert then!" Tracey exclaimed, huffing under her breath. She smirked, secretly trying to impress the others in the group. Xavier cast a lingering gaze at Tracey, slightly agitated by her attempts to diminish his views.

7.

Tyresse, nicknamed *'Ty'*, was a sensitive young man. His Taurian nature induced passion, humility, reliability and patience. He related well to the opposite sex by default of his upbringing, coupled with his nature. Ty grew up immersed in the stronghold of matriarchal figures who nurtured a strong sense of family values. In part, these traits unwittingly enhanced his loving and caring nature which intoxicated lovers and friends alike. Ty's alluring nature and heightened sensitivity created a feeling of security and contentment in those who were close to him.

His family had recently moved to Hainault. However, Ty had grown up in Enfield, raised by his mother Brenda, who strived to emulate and model the work ethics of her own parents while battling with Ty's unethical scruples of being *'on road.'* Brenda tirelessly attempted to reason with her son as he fought his internal struggles to balance his loyalties between his family and the streets.

Brenda thought about having strained to sharpen her wits as Ty's shady activities increased. The bonded love between them was her one and only weapon to impact on his conscience. She clawed with all her might when instinctively aware of danger looming, by encouraging her 17- year old son to stay in the confines of home and watch movies together and creating any distraction which harnessed safety. The fear of loss and uncertainty caused her to feel numb and at times left her panting for breath.

She recalled occasions when she would breathe sharply through her nostrils as she paced her living room floor, repeatedly thumping her clenched fist into the opposite palm, powerless to prevent the streets from encroaching on her life, her home, her son; yet having to painfully accept that Ty was representative of the problems propagated by the gang activity she resented.

Brenda thought back to the times when she held her breath, her eyes darting to the hallway as the key turned in the lock. The relief she felt knowing he was safe was overwhelming; then feeling exhausted once the adrenaline drained away and she needed to sleep. Not wanting to be exposed, she would calmly say, "You home Ty?" exhaling slowly.

Ty would acknowledge her, raising his eyebrows, "Yea, Mum, you alright?"

Brenda would muster a smile, "Yes son, I am fine."

8.

Tyresse had studied photography at a local college in South London before graduating to study photography at fashion Arts College. As time passed, he became more determined and focused on developing his artistic goals.

The more Tyresse strived to succeed, the more he exerted equal pressure to recant past habits which had exalted deviant tendencies, threatening his personal liberty and capacities. The realisation of the tasks ahead of him, although challenging, prompted his fighting spirit, which was to fully embrace his current life choices.

Within the charged group seminar, Tyresse was determined to make a good impression. He was 22 years old and ready to make his mark.

Tyresse had noted the authority with which the ultra slim young woman across the room had addressed Xavier and asked her name.

"Tracey!" cocking her head slightly to the side whilst raising the side of her upper lip, exposing her top incisor.

Tyresse with a broad smile, "I'm Tyresse. Do you have a view about image versus reality TV?"

Tracey responded quickly, "To tell the truth, the way you look and the way you speak determines how successful you are likely to be. It's not what you know, it's who you know, especially in that industry." She quickly added, "Reality TV, I mean."

Tyresse interjected, "So, what of your image?" he paused, with his index finger lightly poised on his chin, moistening his lips as he scrutinised Tracey from head to foot. "Makeup, tanned skin, in September, slick hairdo and fashion accessories, what impression do you want to give?"

Tracey threw her head up and blew out to avoid a flushed feeling coming over her. She was on the offensive, determined not to be defeated, "I am an individual, I'm able to express myself, and I'm comfortable with the way I am. I am sure you are; however, that depends on what you want other people to see." Tracey blew out again through tense lips, conscious that she had exposed herself on the offensive.

Tia cut in, "My attitude and approach tells you not to mess with me." Tia was on a roll, "Image, is what you want it to be." Tia's eyebrows knitted and her hands were now animated in her efforts to express herself.

"Yeah," uttered Tracey, "Image is what you want people to see, isn't it?" She then added, "The media are in the business of sensationalising stuff, making life appear more glamorous than it really is, I reckon."

"Yea, I suppose so," added Tia, "Reality TV allows you to see the characters for who they really are," she smirks. "Those stars are supposed to be our role models, showing us good behaviour, the ideal lifestyle." She looks around the room. "Right?"

Aarti, now agitated, joins the conversation. "Image isn't always what it is meant to be. It may be a lie; a pretence. Reality TV, showing rich women prancing about, wrapped up in their own self- importance and arrogance, it demeans the plight of oppressed women around the world."

Tracey pondered on Aarti's statement, trying to imagine not being able to express her individuality through any image she desired to create. Tracey grabbed on to the idea that image was an essential part of her own persona.

Tracey then leaned forward, poised to attack, when Xavier broke the tense atmosphere by saying, "Image is dead! No one really believes the facade. The stark reality observed in the world's economic climate exposes what is truly unobtainable to the masses; this façade is, in part to blame for inducing crime, and is compounded by festering frustrations, all in an effort to obtain riches."

Tracey looked over at Xavier, "Well you're alright, look at how chic you look today in a designer shirt and boots." She then concluded by questioning "What's that about?" tossing her eyebrows upwards.

Xavier, sensing her measured aggravation, stated, "What is this really about?" Looking wide-eyed over at Tyresse, "As you have been trying to point out, ultimately power and control, steering and influencing the masses; no one is really encouraged to be who they really are, are they?"

The room then erupted with sound, each member defending their own values and points of view.

9.

Tracey's cast iron will and determination were validated through being born into her extended family who had lived in the locality of Dagenham for two generations. Tracey was born and bred in Dagenham, Essex.

Her grandparents told stories of King George IV's era; working in the Mile End Road as tailors. Her mother was a seamstress in Philpot Street, Whitechapel in the 1950s. Uncle Harry, her father's older brother, often boasted about being acquainted with notorious characters; twin brothers, at his old watering hole, near the Bow Bells. The family later moved out to work at the Ford Motor Company in Dagenham.

Tracey had a strong sense of her cultural and racial identity. She was enmeshed in the rich tapestry of a cockney dialect, historical places, recipes, traditions and lineage that she could probably trace back to the Norman Conquest. She was confident and established in her heritage and sense of belonging.

Tracey was mindful of her appearance and invested time and money to ensure she looked pristine and immaculate every day. This was standard day to day practice, and she followed her beauty regimes religiously. Tracey wore size ten jeans and skipped dinner if she noted a slight convex bulge below her sternum.

She reserved 'La Rouge'; the nickname for her booth at The Spotted Dick on a Friday night and her uncle set up a tab at the bar. Tracey thrived on compliments and was often the centre of attention.

The Conception

It was Monday morning, and Tracey arrived late. The lecture had begun, and she quietly shuffled into her seat. She focused on the split ends of her long blond mane and silently protested about her hair having been over-processed at the salon a fortnight ago.

Throughout the lecture, Tracey's attentions were diverted; thinking about the weekend. She then visualised her sizeable black marble desk in an office in the room at the top of a publishing empire in central London. Tracey wanted to take charge of makeup and wardrobe; dressing models for photo shoots of a famous magazine. She knew she was right for the job and needed others to see her *vision*. Tracey was immersed in straightforward presentation; matching colours, soft-focused lenses; pretty.

10.

It was lunchtime. The canteen was the central hub of social interaction, lively debate and idle gossip.

Tracey peered through the rounded windows of the canteen door and spotted Tyresse talking to Tia and Xavier. She recalled the conversation about image versus reality TV. She was undecided about whether to join them at the table. She sighed, looked around at people rushing through as if at a mainline railway station and diverted her attention back to her class peers in the canteen.

Aarti gently caressed her arm and greeted her as she walked by into the canteen. Tracey resigned and followed her in. They both sat at the table and greeted everyone.

Tyresse complimented Tracey about her shoes. Tracey smiled back. Xavier asked Tracey if she was able to find her way around the college. Tracey feeling patronised said, "Yes." she disengaged eye contact with Xavier and focused her attentions on Tyresse.

Tia stared intently at Tracey; her rival. Tia then stood up and began parading up and down. Tracey wondered if she was performing a native mating dance; swaying to the music playing in the canteen and flexing her arms like loose ribbons. Tia then twirled before coming to a halt in front of Xavier. She was now satisfied that she had captured the attention of both Xavier and Tyresse; laughing, she threw her head backwards, displaying the bulge in her throat. Tia then looked at Tracey and asked her whether she wanted to join her outside for a ciggie. Tracey raised her left eyebrow, sighed and said, "Yeah, let's go."

Tia gripped one arm over the other and shuddered whilst drawing on a cigarette outside the building. She had bought a packet of cigarettes this morning. This was a luxury considering that she overspent her budget from her student loan. She dismissed the thought, shrugging her shoulders and shaking her head. She then focused her attention on her latest prey. *Defeat and conquer*, she thought. "So, Tray, can I call you Tray?"

Tracey paused before answering, "My friends call me Tiger, but you can call me Tracey." Tia smirked staring into the road thinking, *So you think you're badder than me. Really! OK.* Tia then looked at Tracey, who was drawing on her cigarette while observing passers-by.

Tia then asked Tracey, "So what area you from?"

"Dagenham." Came the answer, "You?"

"Essex."

"Coming!" Tracey declared, stamping out her cigarette on the ground. Tia, caught unawares, cast her eyes back towards Tracey who was swiping her pass at the barriers. Tia was slightly annoyed. She felt that Tracey had gotten the better of her. Again, she felt vulnerable; the underdog. She had been outwitted by her prey. Tia developed an instant dislike of Tracey.

In an instant, Tia was transported to the dinner hall in her ever-present past. She was standing alone; she was the new girl; 8 years old. She was looking down at her white socks. She was transfixed, avoiding the glare of the other pupils staring at her. She resented being the outsider.

Her insecurities about her identity, life experiences and interpersonal relationships came flooding back. She felt a sharp pain in her chest. Tia then shrugged off the trance-like state she had tumbled into and slowly filed in behind Tracey at the college entry barriers; lying low, prowling, waiting for an opportunity to pounce and devour.

She fought back her emotions when Tracey pivoted in her step and asked her what class she had next. Tia in the midst of trying to compose herself stated, "PR and Marketing."

When they returned to the canteen, Aarti was sitting quietly, listening to Tyresse and Xavier, who were incessantly chattering about sport. Aarti focused on maintaining her composure amidst the differing social norms to what she was accustomed. She felt a sense of relief, familiarity in numbers, when Tracey and Tia returned.

Both sat alongside her and homed in on the conversation between Tyresse and Xavier. Tracey began engaging in the discussion and Tia started to mock the performance of specific clubs in the premier league. Aarti listened intently in a bid to be included, to be able to participate.

On closer observation, it appeared that the others did not notice she hadn't been speaking and had slowly drifted into deep thought about the arranged marriage her parents were proposing. She recalled the conversation she had with her mother a fortnight ago. Preparations for a formal introduction in December had been arranged when she next had a scheduled break. Aarti did not want to let her parents down as they had been so good to her. They sent her to one of the best schools in the region and gave her a privileged lifestyle, including this opportunity to study in the UK.

Aarti smiled when she thought about the warm and loving relationship she had with her parents. Aarti felt challenged by the ideals she had been taught regarding liberation and emancipation from oppression. What hypocrisy; this ideal had not been personally extended to her.

Aarti began to question whether her father had ever considered whether his ideals in regard to emancipation would likely conflict with cultural traditions. Especially when considering that he consented to his daughter's liberal views. She was now frustrated and trapped in her loyalty to cultural tradition and the freedom to make her own choices.

Aarti looked at the young people around her. They were carefree; free of the responsibility to observe and adhere to the cultural norms she had to. The knot in her stomach tightened; the burden was too much for her to bear.

She then considered that perhaps young people in the western world were ill-equipped to handle the responsibilities of adulthood placed on them so young. The rights of passage, perhaps, had not been earned or duly tested. She interrupted her own thoughts, having assumed the role of judge and jury.

Xavier smiled at her and began clicking his fingers to gain her attention, "What are you thinking about?"

"Nothing," she said, casting her eyes to the left, continuing to look at people passing by.

Aarti then thought about the security afforded to her by way of an arranged marriage. She questioned how this would be in a western society. At home, it was now acceptable if a man's wife wanted to work. She drew a deep sigh, which ached at the back of her throat. She flexed her nostrils and blinked as Tia called out to her, "You OK?"

Aarti nodded gently and said, "Yes," with a slight smile on her face. Aarti then cast her eyes downwards towards the table.

Tia then asked, "How are you settling in?

"Fine," Aarti replied. She was curious about Tia, her ethnicity and cultural practices. Aarti wanted to understand more about Tia's relationship with God.

Tia observed Aarti's awkward address and felt the need to protect and mollycoddle her. Tia did not feel threatened by Aarti's persona. Tia moved her chair closer and asked Aarti if she fancied going out for a drink later. Aarti looked up, widened her eyes and said, "I am meeting with family members later." Her tongue was dry as she lied; Aarti felt uncomfortable as it was customary for her to greet and make others feel welcome. Aarti leaned back in her chair as if to create space between them.

Tia shrugged her shoulders and said, "Don't worry we can go some other time." Aarti hoped her clown-like grin would go undetected, her eyes darted around the table. Xavier was smiling at her. She blushed and looked in the opposite direction, almost unapologetically. Aarti's heart was racing. She straightened up in her chair and cleared her throat.

Tia then leaned forward, brushing her left breast against Xavier's shoulder and asked if he was going out for drinks again this evening. Xavier grunted dismissively with a faint smile and settled his body back in the chair. Tia chuckled to herself, leaning both her elbows on the table and pointing her fingers forward. Tia had a brazen look on her face.

Aarti felt incensed. She resented the way in which Xavier had addressed Tia, yet was drawn towards the tactical way in which Tia used her feminine wiles to attract his attention.

Aarti disliked Xavier's arrogance and lack of sensitivity. She wondered how Tia felt. She was angry for Tia; in fact, angry at Tia for not defending her own honour. Aarti's mind was racing. She caught Xavier's eye and shifted her gaze. Xavier was smiling at her. His poise was cool and relaxed.

Xavier was settling into the new social order, experiencing people from differing nationalities, cultures and social classes. He found Tracey amusing and eventful. In Tyresse he saw as an exotic project to arouse his curiosity.

Tia was the goddess, Aphrodite, arousing primaeval sensations in him, and Aarti was pretty, but not yet significant. He imagined her to be a vine flower weaving its way to the giver of life, the most prominent star of the universe.

Xavier looked around at the individuals sat around him. He was bored, seeking new stimuli. He tried to disguise his frustration behind a fixed smile, which was festering thoughts about his desire to conquer, to dominate.

His mind drifted back to a time when his team won the rugby league cup, and he had everyone pandering to his desires. It felt good to be in control, the sensation made him feel powerful, invincible.

Xavier flirted with the idea of developing a meaningful relationship with Tyresse and marvelled at his chiselled features and physique. He welcomed the chemistry which had formed between the two of them and hoped to discover more of himself through this new found friendship.

11.

The soft moving shadows along the cream landscape captured Tia's imagination. She observed the way the shapes danced a rhythm to the flicker of the candlelight. Tia and Archie were covered with a warm snug duvet, huddled in front of a wall mounted fireplace. They laughed and reminisced about the antics they used to get up to back in the day.

Tia reviewed the past and spoke about her family, who still lived in a huddled cul-de-sac, bordering a notorious housing estate where hoodies, low batties and designer jeans were the latest *'ting on road'. 'On road'*, was the phrase adopted, instead of street, where Tia and her friends would hang out together.

On road, they were able to develop a group identity that they perfected, uninterrupted or corrupted by the trappings of the conformities which enslaved their parents. They formed a sisterhood; a grafted extension of who they deemed as family that they could trust, depend on and truly express themselves with. The sisterhood became Tia's confidantes, mentors, teachers and idols. At the time, her aspirations were invested in them and what they all wanted. On reflection, she realised that this was a collective thought and not her personal ideals.

Reminiscing, Tia began to see that her aspirations needed to be fashioned by her own desires, birthed of her own experiences, dreams and mistakes. She thought she could now see what her destiny looked like and understood her future intentions.

The Conception

Staring into the mirror, Tia admired herself; fantasising about marrying her favourite pop star, dodging the paparazzi and carrying a Chihuahua in her designer handbag.

Tia was one of three children, but her mother's only child out of wedlock. Tia was different, her hair and skin tone were different. Her mother, Faye, kept saying, "You're all the same to me, babe." Tia nevertheless was made to feel different. She never received cuddles, encouragement or praise from the man whom she presumed was her father, until he corrected her casually one day over dinner.

Tia recalled feeling nauseous and overwhelmed with feelings of disbelief and abandonment. She was stunned; unable to speak, afraid to hear those words repeated. Her mother hung her head in shame and refused to acknowledge her gaze.

She remembered running, running through the numerous blocks of flats in a mass of hysteria. She meandered through what seemed like an endless maze of indiscriminate shades of grey. The tall columns seemed to envelop her as she ran to escape them, out towards the open fields close by on the heath. Cold tears streaming down her face, muffled screams caught in the wind on a rebound as she ran past.

Several days had passed, and Tia began to familiarise herself with her surroundings and the college layout. She felt deflated, having sneaked out early during her third week of the new term.

Over the past few years, Tia had developed a habit of speaking to her own conscience.

From an early age, Tia learnt to disbelieve and ignore her instinctive thoughts and responses. It was easier that way. She learnt to manipulate and covet her intentions as a means of survival.

She focused her energies on studying her prey, as a means of distraction, ever conscious of the need to suppress her fears, her anxieties, her unhappiness; just to be still in her mind, to feel numb was to feel free for a while.

Tia wanted to be a fashion designer, creating thought-provoking designs which would capture the imagination of the audience. Tia had sweated tears, exercising perseverance, to complete a year's access course, whilst battling negative thought patterns which had taken root over so many years. She had almost convinced herself that she was not worth fighting for. She then reflected on her dream board and memories of the ever-present demons.

Constance was Tia's hero, her best friend since childhood, who showed her love, affection and loyalty. Constance was a free-spirited and bold creature. She lived around the corner to Tia and had grown up on a bedrock of sweet reggae music, hot chicken soup, curried goat and love in the home.

Tia would observe Constance for hours as she swayed to and fro with the music thumping and Constance screeching at the top of her voice, singing into her worn hairbrush. Tia would laugh, her heart felt warm and safe in Constance's box bedroom at the top of the house. It was always warm, cosy and full of stuffed animals, old and new, as well as interesting artefact's her father had brought home from his travels abroad.

Tia was beginning to spend focused time looking inward and soul-searching; only then would she be able to start to understand what virtues and characteristics she needed to possess. It was only as she began to invest time in understanding herself that she would be able to start discerning aspects of her character which let her down.

Her impulsiveness had more often caused her to make rash decisions contrary to her renewed thinking of exercising patience and thoughtfulness in her decision-making processes. Had she taken the time to think, counting backwards from ten, she may have been able to exercise the discipline and commitment necessary to stay in class each day and work hard towards fulfilling her aspirations, which had once been misguided.

12.

Xavier sat on the fire escape of his second floor flat. His fingers were interlocked, the whites of his knuckles stretched as his grip tightened. He was staring down intently at the alleyway which ran alongside his building.

The veins in his forehead were throbbing, his stomach tied up in knots. He tipped his head back and threw another shot of neat brandy down his throat. He then twirled the glass continuously in his hand before slamming it down on the table, alongside the half-empty 350 ml bottle of vodka.

He stood up and staggered through the open doorway. He cupped his face in his hands and wiped the persistent sweat from his brow and neck. He flexed his shoulders upwards in response to the river of sweat running down his back. He ripped off his shirt and stumbled into his bedroom.

There was a soft but sturdy knock at the front door. Tyresse cracked open the door. "What's up." Tia then enquired whether Xavier was there. It was 2.00am. She wondered why Tyresse was there. He asked her to wait and closed the door gently.

Tia stood back in the hallway and frowned, folding her arms. Five minutes later Tyresse came out and told Tia that Xavier had gone to bed. He began slowly walking down the hallway and beckoned Tia to follow. Tyresse asked her how she had got there. Tia answered, "By bus." She was annoyed that she was unable to speak to Xavier herself. She then asked, "Why didn't you let me talk to Xavier myself?"

Tyresse answered, "He was tired and wanted to sleep."

Back at the flat, Xavier laid across the bed, intoxicated and stripped naked. He was overwhelmed with feelings that he could not comprehend. Xavier felt the bed tremor underneath him. He began to imagine that he was invincible; that he was misunderstood and was consumed with the thought that others had tried to manipulate him for their own unjustifiable causes.

Xavier's thoughts switched. He then thought about his own physique, which he admired. He praised his own efforts to maintain and sustain a healthy mind and body. He thought about his aspirations to become an editor of a designer magazine, where he as the puppeteer, could create and fashion ideals which the masses would embrace and emulate.

He thought people to be ugly and selfish, with hidden agendas they carelessly denied. He despised the old for their ill-gotten status of sovereignty over the young purely by default of their maturity. He considered their views and ideals, outdated and prejudiced against the fresh and unadulterated minds of the young, not having been polluted or corrupted by dated hemmed in philosophies.

Xavier then began to hear numerous voices all around him. He closed his eyes and drifted into sleep.

He woke with a pounding headache and reached for his phone. It was 8.00am. He rolled over, grabbed his head and groaned deeply. "Aaagghh," he sighed and sat on the edge of his bed. *Was Tyresse here last night? How much did I have to drink? :*He thought.

He then stood up, focused his attention on the bathroom and walked straight ahead.

Truthingdom

Xavier wiped the steamed mirror in the bathroom with his robe and smiled at his reflection.

13.

Tyresse was speaking intently on the phone, "Yow, have you got anything?"

Denzil's gruff, muffled voice answered, "What you looking for?"

"AG."

"Yeah, I got dat. Where should I come to?"

"The usual spot; 7 pm."

Denzil answered, "Yeah, Yeah."

Tracey approached Tyresse outside the classroom and said, "You coming to Sally's diner?" Aunt Sally's diner, a cafe in the high street close by to the college, became their local meeting place during break times, or after college. Tyresse declined the invitation as he had already made plans to travel to Enfield.

Tyresse sat huddled in the carriage seat, staring out at the vast white landscape which reflected against the bright skies. He noted the snow blanketed trees and parallel train tracks which ran alongside him. He thought about the transaction; making a profit for himself. He began to calculate, a quarter ounce for £400, split in half, which he could then sell for a profit. He felt cold and pulled his hoodie lower down over his eyebrows and went to sleep as the rain trickled by his head on the opposite side of the glass.

Twenty minutes later he opened his eyes and shrugged his shoulders as he stood up to exit the carriage. He left the station and headed down the high street and meandered through the open air outdoor marketplace, which had been extending out from the indoor market. Christmas was close. Tyresse hadn't been to Enfield in a while. Nevertheless, all seemed familiar. He saw himself reflected in individuals passing by; all differing shades from amber to dark chocolate.

The stalls exhibited an array of fresh, coloured fruit and vegetables, their discarded containers tossed in a pile around the back of the stalls. The butcher stood outside the shop in his stained overalls shouting, "A box of chicken, 33lbs, come and look, ladies, come and look."

Tyresse pulled the zip on the front of his hoodie up towards his Adam's apple and shrugged his shoulders. The market streets were peppered with litter and remnants of foodstuffs. Every corner of the market was teeming with people chattering, a host of different sounds which blended into the thudding reggae music, which came from a side stall. The trader stood bobbing up and down on the spot and rocking his shoulders in time to the beat; his hands were stuffed in his loose fitting jeans and his woolly hat sat partially off his mounting afro.

Utterances were more pronounced the closer Tyresse swerved towards another trader who shouted, "Banana's for a pound." Although unfamiliar with the tribal designs, Tyresse recognised the sharp sun gold yellow fabric woven within a deep blue backdrop, wrapped around the voluptuous waistline of an African woman who was bartering the price of yams with the seller, who was trying to convince her that she was getting a good deal.

Splash, water leapt off the top of the blue tarpaulin which had been forced into a pointed crest by a stick, as the vendor tried to relieve the basin of water swelling above his head on top of the stall. Tyresse veered past to avoid a collision.

Another vendor was stirring a pot of sweet-smelling curry spices which wafted from his mobile van. Tyresse nodded at the man; he recognised Mr D'Abade, a Trinidadian man who lived on the estate close by to Denzil.

Tyresse darted to the left, into a cafe. The cafe was warm. He felt caressed by the warm smells of toasted bread, eggs and strong coffee. Denzil was slouched in a booth; he leaned forward as Tyresse approached him. They slapped hands, greeting one another and began talking.

As the waitress walked away, having taken Tyresse's order, he leaned forward and slid 4 bills to Denzil, who swiftly received the bundle, shoved his hands under the table and peered down at the bundle in his hands. He began counting silently to himself and confirmed the amount was there in full. He then stuffed the cash into his inner jacket pocket and slid the quarter ounce of coke to Tyresse across the table. Tyresse cupped his hand over Denzil's, drew it back and stuffed the small rock wrapped in foil in his jogging bottoms and zipped up the pocket. Tyresse then rubbed the rock lodged inside his pocket to make sure it was there.

"Who's it for?" Denzil asked

"Some guy at college, init," Tyresse replied.

"Careful, you don't know him," Denzil cautioned.

"He's kosher man," Tyresse reassured

"I got beef man, Tall Stacks is on me for readies owed," Denzil confided, "His boys threatened to take me out if I don't come up with the readies."

"How much you owe?" Tyresse now concerned for Denzil.

"Five bags." Denzil sighed. "You know what he told me? If I give up my girl, his boy will accept late payment." He kissed his teeth, "Fucking cheek."

"What you gonna do bruv?"

Denzil sat resigned, "I don't know man."

14.

Three months had passed since the beginning of term. Tia was convinced that Tracey and Aarti were not a threat to what she thought was a monopoly on the men in the group; namely, Tyresse and Xavier.

Tia invested time in perfecting her appearance and enhancing her physical assets. Tia devoted time strategising how to draw both men to her. She would try to manipulate them to conduct her bidding; to have them favour her above the others.

When consciously aware of her calculations, she tried to convince herself that she could not intently be so self-conceited, believing that they would naturally gravitate to what she considered her charming and captivating personality.

Tia loved the companionship of Archie. She enjoyed their conversation and banter. She recognised herself in him: a familiarity which gave her a place of refuge. Tia did not like being alone, she never enjoyed her own company, being left with the sound of her own thoughts and deepest inhibitions.

Only recently, Tia began considering the need to review and explore the meaning or the impact of past experiences. She had not really considered the validity of her conclusive thoughts, resolutions or actions. Tia had only just begun to think how her life experiences, or the impact of others, affected her as an individual.

Tia struggled with trust and had little faith in anyone, least of all Tracey and Aarti. She viewed Tracey as her rival and discounted

Aarti, as a *'freshy'*, who had little understanding of the politics of warring women, plotting for battle.

Secretly Tia admired Tracey's boldness and spontaneity and was busy concocting an antidote to counteract her feelings of inadequacy.

Tia felt the need to protect and defend Aarti, interpreting her silent demeanour for weakness.

Aarti had begun to settle, becoming accustomed to the sights and sounds of the capital city. She was able to relate well with the group, whom she had not yet deemed as friends, only acquaintances. Aarti felt least able to identify with Tia, whom she thought to be gullible and misguided. Nonetheless, she admired Tia's persistence in obtaining or achieving whatever she desired. In some ways, she envied Tia's ignorance, noting her tactlessness and inability to safeguard her own interests. Being fully aware of the responsibilities brought to bear in her own existence.

15.

It was hot, and the club was crowded; music was pumping out, throbbing through the fabric, out of the box. Aarti was consumed by the sights of young women skimpily dressed, expressing themselves freely on and off the dance floor; performing what she thought were creative versions of the *Karma Sutra*. Tia laughed at Aarti's widened stares which at times appeared transfixed, looking at what she considered obscenities performed around her. Several people seemed to be clumsy, throwing themselves around and talking nonsense. Tia explained that they were plastered. "Plastered?" Aarti quizzed.

"Yeah, drunk." Tia replied.

Xavier and Tyresse had arrived earlier and ushered the girls into a side booth which they had reserved. Tracey smiled as she looked around, raising her glass. Xavier poured chilled wine into it. Tia was chatting to Archie and pointing to a girl in the crowd. Tyresse took a sip of beer and began dancing. He moved his hips effortlessly in time to the music. Several girls approached him and formed a circle around him. They started heckling to the sounds of the music. Tyresse appeared to be in his element.

Aarti felt a burning sensation in her chest as the cold fluid travelled to her stomach. She felt a weird sensation as she raised her glass in another toast. She listened to the mesmerising beat of the music. She twirled round and round, the room was spinning. The faces merged into a collage. She heard Tia say, "She needs fresh air."

Aarti was led out of the club. She felt the cool breeze on her face as she staggered out of the doorway. She shivered at the sensation of the breeze; sharply inhaling the night air through her nostrils.

It was dark. Aarti followed her feet forward and felt the pull; she was spun around, lost balance and fell down scraping her knees on the cold coarse surface. She felt a cold blade press against her face. Her hair gripped back; she felt his soft, warm flesh thudding against the back of her throat. She heaved. He grunted and pressed the blade into her cheekbones.

He grabbed her mane and pinned her to the ground. The rainwater hit her face, a searing pain ripped up passed her thighs through her cervix. Her vagina burnt, she could not stop the rhythmic thrusting pangs which ached. She cried out in vain. Her screams muffled, then a numbness set in, paralysing the muscles in her face. Her screams now masked in silence.

She caught a glimpse of a red and yellow dragon moving across the flexed muscles of his inner thighs. She was mesmerised by the deepened shades of red enveloped by clearly defined black ink. The dragons double-edged tongue rippled in motion as he slowed and descended, crushing her as he lay still. Panting in earnest, he shifted his head upwards exposing his neckline. He lifted himself free and staggered away.

Aarti slowly looked around her, the rain softly pattered against her skin. She wept silently to herself, tossing her head to the other side, parallel with the pavement beneath her.

As she exited the club, Tia lit her cigarette, tossing her hair up into a loose ponytail. She could hear a commotion in the street and saw Aarti sat on the edge of the pavement. Tia ran up to her, "What's wrong?"

A young woman said, "I think she's been raped. We called the ambulance and the police."

Tia knelt down in front of Aarti and gently said, "Oh God! Did you see him?"

Aarti slowly shook her head.

16.

Aarti felt sickened by the smell of antiseptic while lying in a hospital bed. The traffic peered through the gaps in the openings of the curtain pulled around the cubicle; exposing her humiliation. A nurse was scribbling notes; Aarti was consumed with thoughts of having been violated. She thought: *Yesterday I was a virgin, pure and untainted. I should not have gone to the club. What if I hadn't had a drink? Who was to blame? I cannot speak of this to my parents.* This was her secret shame.

Tia sat outside Aarti's cubicle, cradling herself. Tia stared into space, excavating buried memories of her initiation into an urban street gang. Tia and several other girls were sexually exploited by older male gang members in order to gain entry into the gang. The older girls within the gang showed little emotion when prepping the younger ones to complete their initiation. Tia learnt that to fulfil this initiation was the difference between being accepted, belonging and being rated as anything important.

Tia pressed her eyes shut when she thought how she manipulated her thoughts to convince herself that she enjoyed it. Performing sexual acts on young men and having unwanted sex with them. Tia had suppressed her own feelings, compromised her personal morality to accommodate the fiendish indulgences of others. Tia then sighed and thought: *I'm OK though. Got through it. It's about payback now.*

Tia then drifted into thoughts about using her sexuality to entrap men. To hurt them the way they had hurt and used her. She then sat up triumphantly; straightened her back and slapped her hands on her lap.

The nurse peered through the curtain and whispered to Tia, "Would you like to come in?" Tia leapt to her feet and entered inside.

Tia moved closer to Aarti. Tia felt awkward, not knowing what to say. Tia was suddenly dumbfounded. She thought: *We have both been abused. What should I say?* Tia walked around the bed and sat close by. Tia and Aarti's eyes met.

Tia then said, "You OK?"

"Yeah," Aarti answered.

Tia felt increasingly uncomfortable, realising Aarti was an unwilling participant and said, "Can I get you anything?"

"No," said Aarti blankly.

Aarti lay motionless, dropping eye contact with Tia. Aarti felt floods of despair. Tia's heartbeat raced. Aarti began heaving and coughing violently. She threw her head off the side of the bed. Her mane tossed forward and hung below her. Tia hurried off her seat and knelt in front of Aarti. Aarti was sobbing. Tia gathered Aarti's mane of hair and helped her to lay back on her pillow.

Tia opened her mouth to speak, but no words came out. Then she uttered, "I am sorry, I am sorry."

Aarti was overwhelmed. She began wailing. Nurses came rushing into the cubicle and made arrangement for Aarti to be transferred to a side room.

Tia was unsure how to console Aarti, so she stepped back to allow the nurses to comfort her. Tia felt lost, unequipped and unable to deal with the situation. She thought about whether she should know what to do. One woman to another: *Should I know? What can I do?* Tia edged backwards. Tia asked the nurse to tell Aarti that she would be back later.

Tia then walked away; with each step, she felt the weight had been lifted. She felt uneasy about her mixed and guarded feelings, as well as her inept response to what was an intense situation. Nevertheless, she was eager to repack her jumbled feelings and increased her swagger with every motion of the hips as she left the hospital wing.

Aarti sat staring in front of her. She took a long deep breath and fed the breath out between her tensed lips. She was relieved that Tia had left the cubicle as she felt her awkwardness.

A firm voice said, "Hello there." Aarti focused her gaze on a female police officer who was slowly walking towards her bedside escorted by a nurse who stood silently close by.

"Hi," whispered Aarti.

The police officer explained to Aarti that she had brought a SAFE (sexual assault forensic evidence) kit, as they would need to gather evidence to help identify the perpetrator and in order to prosecute. Aarti's heartbeat raced, and her breathing laboured as she listened. She looked around and saw no one. Tia had gone, and she felt so alone; exposed. She did not want to be left alone and wondered when Tia had left. Aarti had no concept of time just pain and despair.

The police officer explained what the kit consisted of and what she would do. The nurse gently rubbed Aarti's arm and reassured her that it was OK. Aarti had blocked out most of what was being said and focused her gaze at the end of the bed. She did; however, hear herself say, "OK" and became immediately enraged, drew back her arm and cuddled herself. The policewoman leant forward and gently said, "Are you ready?" Aarti laid back and began to whimper gently, with her head turned away, as the nurse swabbed her vagina. She wanted to die; to stop conscious thought. She felt violated all over again.

Aarti tried hard to concentrate; to remember what had happened. She was unable to answer many of the questions asked by the police. She felt agitated not being able to remember. Not being able to keep herself safe. Getting drunk. She had dropped her guard. She was angry with herself. Questions resounded in her head: *Why did I go? Why did I drink? Why? Why? Why?*

17.

Tracey stretched her arm from underneath the quilt and grabbed her mobile phone perched on the edge of the side cabinet. She noted numerous messages logged on her phone from Tia. Startled, she sat up. "Oh my God," Tracey read: AARTI'S BEEN RAPED. WE ARE AT QUEEN MARY'S NOW. Tracey gasped and covered her mouth with the palm of her hand. She began to dial frantically.

Tia answered in a lowered voice. "You saw my messages."

"Yeah… Do the police know who did it?"

"No, no they don't," came Tia's response.

There was an awkward silence.

Tia then informed Tracey that she was collecting Aarti from hospital today.

Tracey interjected, "Oh, so they are releasing her today?"

"Probably."

"So, you're not sure."

"No, not really."

After another awkward silence, Tracey then asked, "Has anyone spoken to her family?"

Tia hesitated, "Ah, No...Where were you last night? I looked around for you, and you weren't there."

Tracey then blushed saying, "Yeah. I wasn't feeling well, so I went home early." Again, there was an awkward silence. Tracey and Tia agreed to meet at the hospital at 14.00 hours.

As Tracey laid back, she observed the quilt covered mound surfacing beside her and looked away feeling guilty that she had not been there. She wondered if this would have happened if she had been there last night. She wondered if she would be considered selfish and lustful for leaving without ensuring Aarti got home safely. She then cut her thinking mid flow and said, "Tia was there."

Tracey then slowly walked into the bathroom and closed the bathroom door. Tracey tried to muffle the sounds as she heaved into the toilet bowl while tightly clutching her stomach.

Back at her own bedsit, Tia slumped back in the chair, staring into space. She thought about the physical and mental torment Aarti might be suffering. Her mind then drifted back to a time when she jested and befriended those who violated her as their given rights on the streets.

She recalled containing her frustration and her feelings of anger when kneeling in front of the older ones; being jeered to perform perverted acts against her own will; unable to voice her disapproval. She then felt repulsed by herself. Angry that she had not stood up for herself. She lost her innocence to the prey of lust. She felt confused, however, needing acceptance at that time. Tia still needed to be loved and to understand how to receive love. Tia cuddled up to Archie who was sitting on the sofa watching TV.

It was 2:15 pm, and Tracey had arrived on time. She spotted Tia walking towards the hospital entrance and pointed at her watch. Tia began to apologise. Tracey stared blankly at her and began walking towards the lift. They were both silent as the lift doors opened and stepped onto the ward. Tia led the way. On entering the room, Aarti was lying on her side, looking away from them, towards the window. Tracey walked around the bed and sat parallel to Aarti's face. She smiled at Aarti and gently rested the refreshments on the side table.

Tracey maintained eye contact with Aarti and asked her how she was feeling. Aarti cleared her throat and said, "I don't know. I feel numb."

Tracey then said, "Tia's here." Aarti smiled; however, she did not look behind her. Tracey beckoned Tia to walk around the bed. Tia did this quickly, as if grateful for instruction. Tracey then explained that she had a headache and left the club early. She didn't mention that she had not gone home alone. Tia observed that Tracey appeared confident addressing Aarti. There was an element of control girding the frailty of the situation. Tracey spoke while both Aarti and Tia listened. Both felt safe, able to settle behind Tracey's boldness.

After two hours, Tracey reassured Aarti that she would return to escort her home in the morning and would spend some time settling her back at home. Tia remained silent.

Aarti sighed a sigh of relief, having engaged with Tracey while maintaining eye contact. This was a massive effort for her as she felt unable to verbally respond. At times, when Aarti felt compelled to speak to Tracey, she felt a gripping sensation in her chest, constricting when she panicked. It ached and exhausted her.

Later that evening, when ward rounds had been completed, Aarti had been told that she would be discharged. As Aarti lay in bed, her mind drifted to thoughts about travelling to India in a week's time for the holidays, and she had arranged to meet her prospective husband during her visit.

Aarti was thrown into disarray, vague about what she should do. She began crying. She then prayed for peace and comfort. Soon afterwards she fell fast asleep.

18.

Xavier threw his hands open as he gestured to Tyresse across the classroom and mimed, *Where's Tracey and Aarti?* Tyresse shook his head from right to left. Tyresse glanced across at Tia who appeared distracted, staring down at her desk.

During the lunch break, Xavier and Tyresse approached Tia in the dining hall. She was sitting by herself, tapping an unlit cigarette on the table. Tyresse moved closer and asked Tia if she was OK. Xavier sat opposite, scrutinising Tia closely.

Tia straightened in her seat. She denied knowing where Tracey and Aarti were and said that she wasn't feeling well, and both accepted her explanation.

Tia then asked them where they were as she recalled that neither were present to witness what had happened to Aarti over the weekend. Both seemed reluctant to say where they had gone to. Tia was slightly annoyed by this and excused herself from the table.

Tia then turned back and asked Xavier if he was OK the other night, as Tyresse would not let her into his flat. Tyresse noted Tia's beckoning stare and Xavier's controlled response. "I was busy."

Tia hurled her eyes at him, looking at him from the top of his head to his feet and then walked away. Tia cast away the thoughts of rejection and walked out of the college onto the pavement. She walked over to the bus stop and headed to Aarti's bedsit in Kentish Town.

Tracey cracked the door, "Oh it's you." Tia slid around the door and whispered asking if Aarti was alright. Tracey nodded quickly. They walked up the stairs into Aarti's spacious bedsit on the top floor. Tia greeted Aarti with a nod and informed them that the guys had been asking for them. Aarti looked worried. Tia noted this and said, "But I told them I didn't know what had happened to either of you." Aarti looked relieved.

Tracey raised her eyebrows and said, "Well, it's none of their business, anyway."

Aarti looked anxiously at Tracey who stood up and said, "So, who wants tea then?"

Tia said "Yes." She then looked across at Aarti, who nodded slightly. Tia dreaded being alone with Aarti as she did not know what to say.

Tia then said, "Did you sleep much last night?"

Aarti lied, "Yeah," looking expectantly toward the door.

Tia then sat awkwardly on the edge of her seat. She then stood up and said, "Where were those guys on Saturday night?"

Aarti shot a glance at Tia and said, "I don't know." Tia then began to explain that neither had disclosed where they were. Tia just wanted to deflect from the silence. Tracey then entered the room with two cups of tea. Aarti was holding her chest. Tracey asked what was wrong, resting the cups down and walked over to Aarti who said, "Xavier and Tyresse were not there. Where did they go? They were supposed to be with us."

Tracey then said, "I don't know; hey let's not worry about that. Let's focus on getting you better, OK?" Aarti leaned into Tracey, while Tia sat wondering where those guys had gone to.

Tracey decided to stay the night as Aarti had expressed her fears of being alone. Tia felt disheartened and travelled to Xavier's flat that evening. She found Tyresse there. The two were having dinner when she arrived. "Thanks for the invite," she said. Xavier offered her his plate. Tia laughed and asked if she could scramble some eggs. The aroma soon filled the space, along with toasted bread and butter.

Tia then sat amongst them, determined to deter them from the video game they had set up on TV. She began to question their whereabouts on Saturday night. She accused them both of abandoning the girls, considering they were all meant to be raving together. Xavier stated that he was not obligated to escort them home after the club. Tyresse agreed, saying that neither of them was responsible. Furthermore, they were young women capable of looking after themselves. Tia purposely dismissed their responses and lit a cigarette.

Xavier prepared a roll up. The aroma of marijuana gripped the atmosphere and filled the room. Tia smiled as he passed the joint around. As Tyresse pulled on the joint, he moved the smoke around his mouth. Tia asked how it made him feel. Tyresse stated that it made him feel mellow. Tyresse, however, thought about occasions when he blacked out or just slept like a nocturnal creature all day and was wide awake at night.

Tyresse recalled that his mother persistently complained about how docile and unresponsive he became when he smoked dope. Sleeping all day instead of looking for work or going to college. Trying to get him out of bed every morning by any means was a real struggle. She would beg him to seek medical help to address his insomnia. Tyresse thought about the occasions when his mother Brenda had even expressed concern about his paranoid behaviour.

Tyresse would feel a way when his mother became upset; telling him about his acute rages when he ran out of weed. She described how he would switch; his eyes darting from left to right, turning his room upside down and accusing her of throwing away his drugs or his friends stealing from him.

Tyresse did admit that he found it difficult to sleep, and that *'weed'* made him relaxed, not docile. He found it more difficult; however, to relate to being described as paranoid. He was of the opinion that he was just upset because he couldn't find his *'tings'*.

Tyresse had a close relationship with his mother, who had raised him as a single parent. He was a bright and pleasant child who enjoyed the company of others and felt comfortable within his immediate and extended family.

Tyresse thought his mother was a strong woman of good moral character and ambition. She had studied hard and become a professional, earning a good salary. Tyresse observed her consistency every day, getting up to go to work, keeping house, providing food for the table and clothing him.

Tyresse enjoyed attending infant school and formed positive relationships with others. Secondary school was an education in itself. The school playground taught him the entrepreneurial spirit. Young girls set up shop in the toilets offering a rinse and braids for £15 at lunchtime. Young boys bartered the price of skunk and trainers from off the back of a lorry. Business was good. Tyresse was lured by the *'haves'* as opposed to the *'have not's'* and learned to decipher the grade of weed on sale.

Tyresse became part of the warring factions associated with the postcode battles; walking in numbers to avoid being jumped by rival hood rats; understanding honour amongst thieves; *snitching* was considered sacrilege.

Truthingdom

Tyresse fell out of his daydream and focused on his surroundings. Xavier had fallen asleep on the sofa, and Tia was singing to music on her mobile phone.

Tyresse sprung to his feet, said goodnight to Tia and left. The night air was cold. Tyresse caught his breath, huddled his clothing around his neck and walked briskly out into the night.

19.

Tracey looked into the mirror at her reflection. She looked pale. She cuddled her midriff and examined her cheekbones. "Round, I look like a plum," she said sucking in her cheekbones. She then stroked her throat gently and began brushing her teeth. They looked a little chalky. She felt tired, "I need energy."

It was Sunday morning, and Tracey was going home for lunch with her parents. She often went back on a Sunday to meet up with the family.

She arrived 20 minutes earlier than usual as she wanted to talk to her mother on her own.

"You OK darling?" her mother said. "I can always tell when you have something on your mind." This fact annoyed Tracey slightly.

"I am seeing someone," Tracey muttered.

"Really" her mum replied.

"Yeah," Tracey said hesitantly.

Carol was pottering about the kitchen putting the final touches to lunch. Tracey tried to get her attention when her father walked into the kitchen.

"Hello babe, you OK?"

"Fine Dad," Tracey said hurriedly, trying to hide her impatience.

Dave grabbed a beer out of the fridge and walked into the living room.

"What's up?" Carol said.

"You're bursting to tell me; what's wrong?" Carol now stood facing Tracey with her hand on her hip. Tracey blushed and looked down at the black marble work surface.

"I'm dating a black guy,"

"Woow!" Carol said laughing. "Your dad's going to love that!"

Tracey exhaled and shut her eyes. Carol now began to organise the cutlery around the kitchen table. Tracey opened the cupboard and took out the plates. She then slowly began setting them on the table.

Dave was the last to sit at the table. Tracey began dishing out the vegetables.

Dave sat back. "So, how's tricks?"

"Hard," Tracey replied.

"You don't know what hard is, girl," Dave chuckled. "When I was young..." Dave then began speaking about the past. Tracey looked at her mother who was staring back at her smiling. Tracey was building up the courage to tell her father about her Tyresse. She huddled herself in the chair and took a deep breath.

"Dad,"

"Don't tell me you've had enough already," Dave interrupted. He continued, "We paid good money to send you there."

"No, it's fine," Tracey said through gritted teeth.

"We've spent enough money on one hair-brained scheme after another," Dave now unapologetic.

Over the years, Tracey's parents had invested in several projects Tracey had become involved in, then abandoned for another. Defeated, Tracey picked up her fork and stabbed a potato. She suddenly felt nauseous and twisted the fork. She became full of self-doubt and engulfed with feelings of disillusionment. She was unable to present a counter argument or explanation which justified her past actions. Her frustration was overwhelming.

Carol sat silently rearranging the food dishes around the table. She then asked, "Tray, would you like some gravy?"

"No thanks, Mum."

Tracey noted Dave heartily stuffing food into his mouth, unperturbed by the change of mood. Carol looked at Tracey remorsefully. This annoyed Tracey as her mother always played the scapegoat for her father's actions.

Tracey grew up in a home where her father beat her mother. This happened more often at the weekend or on payday when he came home drunk and or spent his wage packet before he got home. Tracey took her brother upstairs when their parents argued. At times she would strain her ears to listen to the muffled sounds through the bedroom wall.

Mum would wear heavier make up or stay indoors for extended periods until the bruising disappeared. Social care became involved on one occasion, as Vincent, her brother, had told a teacher, "Daddy hit Mummy and pushed her to the kitchen floor."

Tracey was thankful social care had closed the case following their initial investigations. It was a social stigma to be involved with social care. She thought them to be nosy busybodies who separated families and pretended to care. She knew of a few families who were involved with social care when she was a child. Nevertheless, it was a secret shame, and no one accepted that social services were trying to support families in their local community. Tracey, however, knew some families who needed help; but the community, the collective, would have argued the difference to save face, although knowing they had failed or neglected to provide appropriate care for their children. She knew better now.

Tracey watched as her mother poured the gravy over her sliced roast lamb. Tracey excused herself from the table and went to the toilet. She slumped herself over the toilet bowl and began heaving. She then stood on the scales in the bathroom. Tracey weighed 8 stones 2lbs. Tracey knew that this weight bordered what was considered unhealthy. She was 5ft 6ins tall and had a very slender frame. She touched her collar, and hip bones flattened the front of her dress and went back to the kitchen.

Tracey complained of a stomach ache and retired to the living room. She was unable to tell her dad that she was dating Tyresse. She realised that she was not prepared for his reaction. She did not want to have to explain herself or justify her choices. She had independent thought; she was grown up.

Carol came into the living room. "Cuppa tea, Tray?"

"No thanks, Mum,"

Carol persisted, "You going to talk to him?"

"No," Tracey replied, shaking her head loosely.

Tracey wondered: *Is it was worth mentioning that I'm dating Tyresse. Would it last? Was it a fling?*

Was it really worth the aggravation of mentioning it?

Tracey then thought about why it was important to tell him. Tracey wanted the approval from her parents. Was that a weakness? Did that leave her vulnerable; allowing others to shape her decisions, her thinking? Tracey sank her head between her knees.

Her dad was very patriotic, proud of his country and the monarchy. Although Tracey never thought deeply about patriotism as a word, she acknowledged that she was genuinely rooted culturally and proud of who she was.

Tracey was frustrated that she was unable to say what she wanted to say. However, she accepted that she had to own this weakness. Her father never felt restricted and said precisely what he wanted to say. He never ever considered the repercussions of his actions; railroading through people's lives.

Tracey, on the other hand, lived the harsh realities of his actions and was fully aware of the impact on others. His ignorance and short-sightedness disappointed Tracey, who felt unable to confide in him. His family excused his behaviour saying, "Well that's his way," and "That's our Dave."

Carol resigned herself to the onslaught of his wrath early on in the marriage. Battered into submission, Carol developed a false sense of security, believing that her challenges or contradicting views provoked him to anger, so she just accepted his authority. This, in turn, she thought, would abate his fury.

Tracey had given up trying to convince her mother that her relationship with her dad was supposed to accommodate and fulfil the needs of both people. Although her mother agreed in principle, practice was something very different. Tracey recognised that her mother was caught up in an abusive cycle, indirectly or directly reinforced by his family. Her parents' behaviour was entrenched, and her mother lacked the skills and tenacity to change the habit of what was a lifetime.

Tracey felt defeated looking out at the buildings rushing past whilst sitting on the train. She was troubled by the fact that her dad was racist, but more so about the fact that she was unable to speak her mind without feeling intimidated by him. Why did she allow those feelings of inadequacy to be evoked in her?

On the way home, Tracey stopped at a delicatessen and bought cakes, biscuits, chocolates and sweets. At home, she sat in front of the TV and ate everything she had bought. She felt engorged; sick to her stomach. She got up and ran to the bathroom, slumped over the toilet bowl and began to vomit.

20.

Aarti woke up to the sound of her mobile phone. Day Six! She was tormented by visions of what had happened last weekend. Her parents were calling from India.

"Hi Maa, how you doing?" Aarti cleared her throat. Both her parents peered into the camera.

"Bapuji," Aarti affectionately called her father, "You OK?" She smiled at her father. He replied, "Fine *Beti*."

Her mother then pounced further forward and said, "What time are you landing on the 22nd?"

Aarti replied, "Ah, about 3 in the afternoon."

The school term was now over for Christmas and Aarti hadn't even packed. She was travelling in three days.

"Beti, I have arranged everything! His family cannot wait to meet you," Maa continued. Her father sat still, casting his eyes over his wife's shoulder every so often. Aarti's mother hurriedly kept on talking in her excitement about the arrangements for the pre-nuptial meeting.

Aarti listened quietly, hoping she would not have to speak. "Maa, I have something on the fire," she continued "I will call you with all the details before I fly, OK."

"Oh, OK," her mother said, put off by Aarti's untimely interruption.

"Goodbye for now Bapuji," Aarti said. Her father slowly bowed his head and hurriedly cut the call.

Aarti then blew a sigh of relief. How was she going to cope in India? Her mother was stifling.

Aarti ached all over. She slowly reached for the airmail letter on the side table and pulled out the photo of her prospective husband. She studied the man in the photo. He was just a man in a picture, nothing special.

Aarti threw the photo on the floor and braced herself. She felt desperately sad, overwhelmed by her feelings of hopelessness and emptiness. She felt numb, her skin felt cold. She then began to shiver. She was consumed with feelings of grief; her virginity had been torn away. These thoughts were compounded by the fact that she was destined to marry a virtual stranger, who would then violate her again and again and again. She was now crouched on the floor, crying out loud. She felt the gods had no mercy as she remained trapped in her torment. She wanted to have a shower; to cleanse herself but could not find the energy to get up. Her head was spinning round and round.

Aarti was laying on the floor. She did not know how long she had been there. She pulled herself to her feet and answered the phone, "Hello."

"Hello Aarti, this is Kathy calling from victim support. We spoke on Wednesday, and I agreed to call back later in the week." Kathy spoke to Aarti about their counselling services for victims of rape. Kathy attempted to reassure Aarti that they were there to support her through her ordeal. Aarti just listened; wanting to withdraw from the conversation. Kathy inquired about how she was feeling and offered two appointment dates for Aarti to attend counselling sessions.

Aarti briefly explained that she was going away and agreed to contact Kathy when she returned. She hung up and looked up at the ceiling. She felt exposed; people accessing her personal space. She switched off her mobile phone, drew her curtains and climbed back into bed. It was 4 pm in the afternoon, and Aarti had not eaten.

21.

Xavier caught the train. He was travelling home to his parents for the holidays. He had spent the last few nights finishing off assignments until the early hours of the morning and welcomed the timely break. He laid the back of his head on the headrest and closed his eyes.

"Waterloo! All stations to Hampshire leaving in 2 minutes," came a voice crackling through the loudspeaker at the station.

Xavier pulled his trilby onto the bridge of his nose, stretched his legs and drifted off to sleep.

He stirred between stations, unable to get comfortable. Finally, he arrived at his destination. Hampshire, one of the most beautiful and wealthiest parts of the country.

His parents' holiday home; a detached lodge set in a tranquil backdrop of expansive woodlands, close to a small brook. His bedroom still looked the same. Grade two listed, coloured paint; complimented by floral linen bedding and curtains, solid oak wood flooring and an antique study desk in the corner near the window.

A sense of loneliness gripped him as he stood in the centre of the room. The silence, like chimes ringing in his ears, the stillness airy and haunting. His parents called this place utopia; a place away from the rat race. Xavier was never convinced. Other than boarding school, this was home as a child. The place where he fantasised about having a big family; brothers and sisters to open presents with on Christmas morning; to play with in the woods; to share his father's wrath.

Instead, he cut worms in half, shot stones at squirrels and birds' nests with his wooden slingshot. He thought of the pleasure he derived when hitting his target. He observed their laboured breath fading into stillness. He was ensnared by the frozen expression in their eyes and the beauty of their form.

Xavier never considered the negative impact of his actions or felt remorse. He did, however, feel victorious, having conquered, defeated and destroyed his prey. Xavier never explored his feelings or questioned why he behaved or reacted in that way.

Xavier sat upstairs in his room for nearly an hour before joining his parent's downstairs. His father was in the lounge reading and his mother in the kitchen preparing dinner. Xavier poured himself and his mother a glass of wine. She gratefully received it and took a sip. She took another sip before putting her glass down.

"How was your trip?" his mother asked.

"It was OK, thanks," Xavier replied. "How are you mother?"

"Well, alive," His mother responded.

She then enquired about college and asked Xavier if he had made any friends. Xavier did not make much of an effort to answer, as his mother was preoccupied pottering around the kitchen, not alert to his responses.

Xavier wandered into the lounge where he smelt the aroma of his father's malt whisky. Xavier knew this was his favourite. His father was listening to the radio. Xavier approached him slowly and said, "So father, how's business?"

"Good," His father answered, in a clear, brisk voice. "And your studies?"

"Good," Xavier responded. The two men then sat quietly listening to the radio.

Xavier's mother cut into the silence, "I'll be serving tea and scones shortly." Xavier wondered if his mother was oblivious to the prolonged silences or if she welcomed them. He observed her as she nattered away to herself whilst placing the tea tray on the dining table. His father seemed uninterested in what she was saying, and neither of them made an effort to engage with her. They just sat.

Later that evening, after dinner, they all sat in the lounge and listened to classical music by the log fire Xavier's father had prepared. Xavier stared into the flickering flame which caressed the dark velvet glow around it. His eye then caught the light reflecting off a bronze cup sat on the mantelpiece and recalled memories of holding that rugby cup as team captain in the sixth form.

Xavier noted that his father appeared consumed with his own thoughts and his mother was slowly twirling her glass of mulled wine. Neither of them conversed. It was apparent that this had become a way of life and neither challenged or protested about the level of disengagement which had developed between them. Xavier felt the anger rising inside of him. Not only had they forsaken him long ago, they now abandoned each other. He almost sprung out of his chair.

This alerted his mother who said, "Are you, alright dear?"

"Yes mother, I'm fine."

Xavier then excused himself and went upstairs. He fumbled around in his rucksack. He pulled out a small bag of white powder and clumsily tried to open the zip. Carefully he tapped the bag creating a fine white line on the top of his side cabinet by his bedside, pressed his nose against the wood grain and snorted the white substance. He then laid back on his bed.

There was a knock at the door. Xavier sprang up and looked back. It was his mother, "Good night son."

"Good night mother," As she shut the door, he hurriedly glanced back at the side cabinet. White dust particles were scattered on the surface and the bag containing the powder exposed alongside. Xavier grabbed the bag and shoved it under his pillow. His mother had not noticed.

Turning off his bedside lamp, he lay there staring into the dark abyss of night. He compared this with the city lights which penetrated through the window providing a dim ray of light. A sense of revulsion swept over him. Xavier searched his mind to examine why. His eyes searched around in the dark. A resonant feeling of hopelessness engulfed him. He squeezed his eyes shut to block out the nothingness he felt. In his frustration, he threw himself forward and sat up on the edge of his bed.

Xavier felt his mouth going numb, his tongue felt heavy. He laughed, phasing in and out of consciousness. He then stood up and wanted to run. He began running on the spot. Xavier incessantly chased the rush, like the first time he snorted cocaine. The more of it he took, the deeper the bottomless pit the following morning.

Xavier was desperate to climb out of his living hell. He was convinced he had a brilliant mind, however, misunderstood; sabotaged from a young age by the oppressed, warped minds of those entrapped within their monotonous existences. Xavier was resentful, angry and vengeful, unable to find a resolution. He found it difficult to process his internal turmoil, stumbling through the quagmire of his own feelings. Nevertheless, he recognised those feelings were buried; in his past.

Xavier stirred as spasms gripped his stomach. The darkness penetrated his soul. The cold dampness pierced his nostrils. He could hear the dripping water on the window sill. The stone brick walls smooth and mossy. He pulled away. The cold night air whistled through the window pane. He could hear his heart pounding; his body trembled violently, waiting to be rescued from himself. Xavier then drifted into nothingness.

The stillness of morning caught him between the twilight zone and reality. Xavier let out a huge groan. He decided to leave for London a day earlier than he planned, on Boxing Day. His dreams only existed outside of this place. A prison without walls.

22.

Tia and Tracey repeatedly knocked on Aarti's front door. Tracey dialled Aarti's number and said, "I told her we were going to be here by 12."

Tia then said, "She might be asleep."

At that moment they heard the door latch, and Aarti stood to the side allowing them to enter.

Aarti slightly grinned and followed them upstairs to the bedsit.

"Have you eaten?" Tracey enquired.

"Not as yet," Aarti whispered back.

Tia stood just inside the doorway of the bedsit. Tracey walked across the room and drew open the curtains. She then turned to look at Aarti who avoided eye contact. Tracey asked again if she had eaten and Aarti repeated that she had not yet eaten. Tracey then asked if she had eaten dinner last night. Aarti said that she had fallen asleep early and not woken up until this morning.

It was apparent that Aarti was not coping well. Shut off from the world, isolating herself from everyone. The room had a musky scent, and Aarti was still in her night clothes in the afternoon. Tia offered to make cups of tea and rummaged around a cupboard looking for biscuits or snacks as a hot drink was too wet without one. Tia noted the cupboards were bare.

"Aarti haven't you got any food in?" Tia asked.

"I haven't been shopping yet," Aarti answered.

All three stood there for a brief moment looking at each other. Tracey then suggested going down to the local cafe for a late breakfast.

They all ordered an English breakfast. Tracey glanced over at Tia. The atmosphere was tense and still. Aarti's eyes were cast down.

Breaking the silence, Tracey rubbed her hands together and asked Aarti, "What time are you leaving tomorrow? Are you packed?"

"Not yet," Aarti answered.

Tracey and Tia stole a second glance at each other.

Tracey then said, "Can we help?" Aarti nodded in agreement.

Tia then said, "Aarti, how are you coping?"

Aarti felt a lump in her throat; unable to respond. Tia and Tracey observed Aarti beginning to hyperventilate. Tracey gently gripped her arm and said, "It's OK, It's OK." Aarti became overwhelmed and started babbling.

Tia leaned into her and said, "Listen, we are here for you, and we are not going anywhere, OK?" Aarti shook her head and became silent.

Aarti then said, "I can't tell my parents what has happened. They want me to get married; I don't know." Aarti began to cry. Fighting past the tears, she spoke about the airmail letters from her parents and her prospective husband. She pressed on about the pressure of having to conform, to live up to her parents and the wider family's expectations and the rejection if she refuses. Tia and Tracey listened intently as she spoke.

Back at the bedsit, all three of them had a more extensive discussion about what Aarti had disclosed in the cafe.

Aarti could hear herself defending the rationale regarding arranged marriages. She spoke of the vetting process and period of courtship, allowing time to be acquainted with one another; this tradition is supported by the respective families.

Aarti spoke of her own parents, who had an arranged marriage and had been together for 29 years. Aarti was stressed at not having had an opportunity to familiarise herself with her prospective husband.

Neither Tia or Tracey, however, were convinced that an arranged marriage was something they would condone.

Above all, Aarti secretly tried to convince herself she wholeheartedly believed an arranged marriage was right for her.

Tia then broached the subject, "Aarti have you been eating?" She added, "You hardly touched breakfast."

Aarti took a deep breath and said, "I just want to forget; to wake up and not remember, to stop reliving what happened."

Tracey comforted her saying, "Time will heal babe." She leaned forward towards Aarti and asked, "Have you seen your GP?"

Aarti looked baffled, "Why?"

"You're sleeping until midday most days. I call you, and you tell me that you haven't eaten." Explained Tracey, "You need to get out of this place; get some fresh air. Anyway, let's help you pack."

Aarti felt lethargic. She had no motivation to do anything, including showering herself, over the past few days. She breathed a sigh of relief when Tracey and Tia left, but grateful they had assisted her to pack for her journey. She promised to bring them back some souvenirs and reassured them that she was going to be OK.

Aarti thought about what Tracey had said: *Am I depressed?* Kathy from victim support had spoken about the possibility of becoming depressed and withdrawn. She looked through the literature Kathy had sent her about Rape Trauma Syndrome and recognised a lot of the symptoms outlined in the pamphlet, such as aches and pains, nausea and vomiting, headaches, sleep deprivation, being tearful and not eating.

Aarti took a deep breath. She felt pangs in her stomach and twisted in pain. Although she felt hunger, she did not have the energy to eat. She made a cup of tea and thought about how she could disguise these symptoms in India. She had no desire to engage with others or put up a facade for the duration of her stay.

On reflection, she was grateful that Tia and Tracey were there to support her. She then thought that maybe it would be a good idea to call the doctor and make an appointment to see a counsellor, to help her understand and sort through her feelings.

Tia and Tracey walked to the train station. Tracey expressed her concerns about leaving Aarti alone. "How is she going to cope in India carrying that burden with her?"

"No idea," Tia responded.

"Who escorted Aarti out of the club that night, Tia?"

With a puzzled look on her face, Tia replied, "I don't know."

They then began to speculate about what might have actually happened.

23.

Tyresse jigged to the chorus; it almost didn't feel like church. The baseline was thumping, the praise and worship team were bobbing from side to side, and the pastor's voice was harmonious, along with the melody of the choir and fine-tuned instruments.

Brenda's hands were pointed to the heavens, and she seemed lost in God's glory. Tyresse looked around him at the congregation who were clapping their hands; tambourines were shaking, and the voluptuous Mrs Juna was swaying every which way in the Spirit, cradled in the arms of Sister Thelma. The church was alive with a chorus of voices, praise and supplications unto the Lord.

Tyresse smiled. This was his community, his wider family. The older parishioners knew him as a baby and Brenda had long since been adopted as a spiritual mother.

Each time Tyresse attended church with his mother, his conscience was held to ransom. He felt like a wretched soul, downtrodden and tainted by the dreaded sin he knew too well. He felt guilt-ridden, having spent the previous evening smoking weed until he giggled like a girl; paralytic, slumped in the chair with bloodshot eyes, chasing brandy on ice. "Ahh," he sighed: *It is the weekend, and I'm entitled to relax.*

Brenda touched Ty's shoulder and said, "You OK?" as he appeared lost in his thoughts.

"Yeah, fine Mum." Tyresse watched as his mother prayed, speaking to God as if he was a personal friend and confidante.

Tyresse was slightly envious of the joy she had found in the Lord. She seemed at peace with herself.

Tyresse had agreed to meet Denzil later that day. He needed to pick up some *'food'*. Tyresse enjoyed a roast lunch with his mother and extended family members before heading north.

Denzil's home was as chaotic as usual. His mother, Paulette was perming a client's hair in the living room, while Denzil's two younger siblings were making a mess of their dinner on the carpet. Music was blasting in the background, and two men sat at the kitchen table playing dominoes and jeering each other on.

Tyresse greeted his aunt and mounted the staircase towards Denzil's room, which he shared with his younger brother. Peering out the window, Tyresse observed the obscured skyline, which was peppered with high rise flats and random sounds which rang out into the atmosphere.

Tyresse compared this vista to the ghettoes, otherwise known as the projects, that he had visited as a child in America. As a child, he could not see the resigned souls enveloped by poverty and hopelessness who resided there; the inherent trappings and conscience of social dysfunction. These corridors, which weaved like rabbit warrens, were full of ex-convicts who were ostracised from the economic chain. He thought about the few who rose above their circumstances, to fulfil their own potential.

Tyresse recognised the restlessness which stirred in him; good versus evil. The need to fight, to push forward in order to challenge and beat the odds. This was a real war, waged against inherent racism, the haves and have-nots; glass ceilings etc. To what extent were these hindrances operational? How many of our own self-imposed limitations were influenced by a negative self-image, learnt through the distorted interpretations and/or indoctrination of the supposed wise few?

Tyresse then switched his thoughts to thinking about the future; his future; the destiny he had forged for himself; creating an opportunity to gain new skills; ultimately, to have economic freedom.

Denzil was chattering, almost mumbling under his breath. Tyresse had not made any effort to make sense of what he had been saying. Denzil was now staring at Tyresse. Tyresse raised his eyebrows and waited for Denzil to continue. Denzil continued saying, "What am I gonna do? I owe man dough." He chirped whilst shoving his hand down the back of his side drawer, pulling out an ounce bag of weed and stretching his arm forward towards Tyresse. Tyresse took the bag and gave Denzil two bills.

Tyresse's attitude towards Denzil had changed. Denzil represented the past. Quick, easy money. Tyresse was unsure whether he could change the mentality of a lifetime. Being a nocturnal creature, surfacing at night was a way of life. *Shotting* locally in the streets was a lucrative business which provided the cash; immediate gratification. However, this way of life, potentially, could cost him his liberty or his life.

Her Majesty's Prison was a place where his friends frequented. Friends who struggled to readjust to society once released. They'd been unable to find legitimate work without having to lie and be caught out, having gone through the vetting process. The persistent rejection made the undesirable appear desirable. Returning to the streets was the only option. The need to re-acquire one's self-esteem and respect, as well as one's manhood, the sole control a man on road has left.

Tyresse snapped out of his daydream. The nightmare, however, lived on in the lives of the impoverished living in this local community.

Denzil proceeded to explain that he owed money to the local drug lords, who were now pressing him for payback. Tyresse couldn't help. He was now attending college and far away enough from the streets. Trying to be a success and to better himself. To rise above his own mental and physical trappings. To free himself from the never-ending cycle of poverty and self-induced limitations.

24.

Tyresse slumped into the sofa. He was glad to be home. Brenda was preparing lunch and singing at the top of her voice. Tyresse smiled. He always admired his mum's singing voice. He described her voice as smooth and velvety.

Home was always comfortable; a safe haven away from his mistakes and wrongdoings. A place where he could side-track his responsibilities, knowing that his mother would ensure that the nest was a secure habitat. Tyresse understood that this was wrong. He at times had taken advantage of her protective instincts as a mother, being reliant on her to provide for him at a time when he was unable to make steps to provide for himself.

Tyresse then diverted his thoughts to the first term of the academic year. He was relieved he had accomplished this and looked forward to going back after the Christmas break.

The doorbell rang. It was Tall Stacks, one of Tyresse's friends back in the day. They were tight; close friends. Tyresse had not seen him in a while. They laughed and bantered about pranks and dares they had performed when together in the Square; a location where the *youngers* in the hood met as children. They spoke about the bravery exhibited by one another when confronted by boys from another postcode. They carried knives and knuckle dusters to defend themselves. To protect their honour and their patch from the infiltration of outsiders; rival gangs.

Being initiated into a brotherhood was considered a rite of passage. Coming into adulthood; manhood. They were given respect, recognition and power to rule the streets, to harness short-term economic wealth in the home through the sale of drugs and shifting stolen goods. They were able to finance their superficial lifestyles of grandeur with designer clothes, watches and jewellery.

Tyresse and Tall Stacks then drifted into a more sombre mood; reflecting on the present; hustling to get by on student finances. Tall Stacks was living with his baby mother, unemployed and on benefits.

Both remembered and spoke about lost ones, brothers killed as a result of knife and gun crime. Tyresse remembered his blood-stained tie shirt, drenched with his friend's blood as the life force was expelled from his body. He felt the acute pain, despair and stricken panic as the realisation of death shrouded the atmosphere. Tyresse sighed deeply in order to release the tightening in his chest. He looked across out of the window at the blue sky as a means of lifting the weight of grief he felt. Tyresse gripped his arms around his torso and bowed his head.

Later that evening Brenda approached Tyresse in the lounge. "What's wrong Ty?"

"D would have been twenty-eight this year, Mum."

"Yes," Brenda softly replied. The TV chattered in the background while they both sat in silence, consumed with their own thoughts.

The following morning Tyresse was on the phone talking to Tracey. Tyresse was aware that Aarti was travelling to India and asked Tracey whether she had spoken to Aarti before she left. Tracey explained that Aarti had been exhibiting depressive traits and seemed withdrawn during her visit with Tia yesterday. Tracey said that she was hoping Aarti's trip back home would help to raise her mood.

Tyresse then asked Tracey what time she planned to visit as he had told his mother she was coming for dinner. Tracey giggled, "What time should I come then?"

"About five, six."

Tracey was excited. She thought Tyresse was cool and had swagger. She found him contagious and exotic, like mango fruit juice. Tracey knew he was forbidden fruit, but she was tempted by his masculinity and charm. He was her dirty little secret. Her fantasy lover.

Tyresse stepped into the kitchen and observed his mother as she pottered around getting dinner ready. Her sisters Bertha, Claudette and Samantha were there, as well as four of his younger cousins and Claudette's two grandchildren. They had arrived in their droves twenty minutes ago to assist with the preparations for tonight's dinner.

There was a waft of garlic, curry powder, onions and season pepper in the warm air, which hung over them like a fog. Samantha, Tyresse's youngest aunt, was five years older than him and able to relate to him in a way the others could not. Samantha flung open the back door, and the cool breeze sucked out the haze, which blended with the sweet soca music.

They all laughed, watching Bertha's wide hips sway to the music. Aunt Bertha gripped the huge dutchie pot and stirred that curry mutton like she handled Uncle Johnny, stern with a bit of TLC.

All four women were singing in and out of tune, at times harmonising melodious sounds. They were now laughing and teasing each other. Tyresse stood leaning in the kitchen doorway with his arms folded. He loved the unity exhibited within his family.

The unity of the family was his emotional anchor. In the past, when faced with difficult challenges, Tyresse drew strength from the essence of that unity when having to make life and death decisions on the street. Tyresse was also confronted with this essence when deciding whether to compromise his own life or liberty when faced with the choice of being deviant or committing a criminal act.

This love and unity was the reason he had cheated death or stayed out of prison. His nature, as well as his conscience, prevented him from mastering the killer instinct exhibited by others in the gang he was formerly a part of. Some would tease him for being soft. Nevertheless, they more often spoke to him when emotionally wounded or downcast as he was empathetic and compassionate.

Tyresse's mother pulled him into the kitchen and coaxed him to join them. Tyresse began skanking to the roots reggae music; the women cheered him on. Aunt Bertha then stood in the middle and spun her midriff from side to side with her feet planted firmly on the ground. Claudette bobbed one of her grandchildren on her hip whilst Samantha, and Brenda raised their hands in the air and swayed them in time to the music.

Tyresse whispered to his mum that Tracey was coming at around 5:30, she nodded with a faint smile. Tyresse then climbed the stairs to his room and threw himself on his bed, folded his hands behind his head and lay there thinking about college.

The opportunity to change his life, to re-write destiny. Tyresse was gifted and talented at school. He had the dexterity of mind and was creative with his hands. However, he was prey to sensationalism and pipe dreams. Secretly, he was afraid of failing; of rediscovering contempt again and again through the familiarity of past issues; habitual behaviours which revisited him like a recurring nightmare.

Tyresse looked over at his mobile which was buzzing on the bed. He answered, it was Tracey. She was outside and asking him to let her in.

Tracey looked very elegant with her hair pinned back, wearing a boat neck cream coloured dress which plummeted into an A-line skirt. Tyresse complimented her on her outfit and ushered her into the house. Tracey was flushed, pink in the face having come in from the cold into what seemed like a steam bath.

Tracey whispered, "You sure I look OK?"

Tyresse laughed, "You look fine." He led Tracey into the kitchen. Tracey was overwhelmed by the reception. Samantha and Brenda lunged forward with outstretched hands to greet her, whilst Bertha looked back from the stove and grinned before turning back again.

Brenda introduced Claudette who looked surprised, staring at Tracey through gritted teeth encased by stretched lips. Brenda knitted her eyebrows at Claudette, who then cast her gaze over her own shoulder. Brenda then hurriedly offered Tracey a drink. Brenda then added, "Oh sorry and this is Bertha, my older sister." Bertha glanced behind her and threw her chin in the air, signalling a greeting, then scanning Tracey from head to foot with her eyes. Tracey looked down to see what Bertha was looking at.

Tyresse's younger cousins and Claudette's grandchildren were now huddled around the kitchen door, inquisitive to know who Tracey was. Tracey felt hotter than ever and worried whether her makeup was running down her face. She fanned herself slightly and welcomed the cold glass of white wine. Tracey stared at Tyresse, begging to be rescued. This was overwhelming for Tracey. Yes, she did big families; however, not necessarily all at once and they all seemed to be crammed into the kitchen like nails to a magnet. Tyresse noted her expression and took her into the living room.

Tracey exhaled, looking at the TV. Tyresse patted her hand gently as if to reassure her she would be OK. Tyresse was accustomed to the mini-multitude descending during holiday periods and had become an expert in negotiating space and navigating them away from his room and precious commodities. This did not apply to Tyresse's aunts, however, who were impregnable superwomen you could not deny anything to.

Tracey began to relax, pushing herself further back on the couch. She admired Tyresse's sharp haircut. It made him look more handsome. Tyresse asked Tracey whether Aarti got to the airport on time. Tracey informed Tyresse that she had, however, she expressed her concern about Aarti's low mood and told him that she suggested that she sought counselling support when she returned to England. Tyresse then enquired whether the police made any further headway in determining who had raped her.

Tracey replied, "The police are still trying to gather evidence."

Bertha then waded into the living room and asked Tyresse, without reservation, where Tracey was from.

Tyresse hesitated and said, "Tracey, whereabouts are your family from?"

"Dagenham," answered Tracey, looking up at Bertha, who was standing too close for comfort so that Tracey had to lean back slightly.

"I just wondered," Bertha said and then swayed out of the living room.

Tracey was unsure about her approach and found it quite brash. She then asked Tyresse, "What was that all about?"

"That's how she is, don't worry about it." He tried to reassure her.

Tracey pondered on it before focusing her attention on the children, who were meandering in and out of the room, enjoying themselves and each other's company.

Tracey could not deduce whether she felt animosity from Bertha and felt the need to investigate further, "Tyresse, doesn't she like me?"

"Come on Trace, don't make more of it."

Tracey then felt she had lost the right to express her discomfort on unfamiliar territory and sat defeated. She wondered whether Tyresse was oblivious to her responses or chose to ignore what he could not control.

Everyone was now sitting in the living room when dinner was served. The dining table was too small for everyone, so individuals sat scattered about. Tracey sat close to Tyresse on the couch in case missiles began flying overhead.

Tracey was mindful that she was the odd one out. The white girl in the ring. The children were staring at her as if she was on show at the circus. Tracey was conscious of the efforts Brenda and Samantha had made to make her feel comfortable.

Tracey suddenly began to blow repeatedly out of her mouth. The scotch bonnet peppers in the mutton curry were burning the insides of her mouth. Her chest was on fire, and her ears were itching like mad. She felt like running in any direction until she found a water hole to douse her whole head upside down up to her neck in until the steam had subsided. She began to cough.

Samantha jumped up, "Oh you need some water, hold on." She hurried into the kitchen and brought a tall glass of cool water for Tracey. Tracey gulped down the water as if extinguishing a furnace.

Bertha shouted across the room, "Come up for air love!"

Tracey shot her a glance and thought: *More water between meals wouldn't hurt you either, love.* Tracey sneered as she observed the cellulite folds on Bertha's legs. Tracey caught herself, thankful no one noticed her displeasure.

Tracey offered to help Samantha with dessert. Tracey waltzed over to Bertha, handed her a serviette and said, "How many slices would you like?"

Samantha sniggered, "Oh Lord, you're funny." Samantha then called out to Brenda across the room, "Did you hear that sis; Tracey asked Bertha how many slices of cake she wanted." Samantha was now in stitches. Tyresse bowed and shook his head as if to conceal his laughter.

Bertha said, "No thank you." and kissed her teeth. Her eyes following the plate as Tracey walked away triumphantly to the table, forcing herself not to smile.

Tracey felt victorious, able to hold her own amongst the wilful characters in the room. She became more relaxed as the evening progressed. The sisters eventually became amused with each other and Tracey was able to fade into the background.

Tracey later thanked Tyresse for a warm reception. However, she could not resist protesting very slightly about Aunt Bertha's stern questioning and partial greeting. Tyresse apologised; again, making excuses for his aunt Bertha's presentation. Tracey felt disregarded and disappointed, thinking that Tyresse had trivialised his aunt's tactlessness and rude manner.

Later that night, Tracey stood on the scales in the privacy of her own bathroom. She had gained a pound. Tracey huffed in frustration. She thought back to the evening's events and leaned over the toilet bowl and heaved.

25.

Tracey was furious. How could her father call Tyresse names? "He doesn't even know him," slamming her fists on the table. Tracey was now enraged and demanded, "Mum, what did you say to him?"

Carol then said pitifully, "Tray, I didn't say anything bad, he just lost it."

Tracey took a deep breath and surrendered, "It's OK Mum, don't worry." Carol began crying and sat down at the kitchen table.

Tracey then stood up defiantly, "Where is he?"

Carol responded, "He's gone out babe."

Tracey knew her mother did not have the strength of character to defeat or stand up to her father, but she did. She was no longer a little girl he could intimidate. She was now a young woman able to fend for herself.

As a small child, she had often sat at the top of the stairs listening to her father make her mother beg him to stop beating her. Tracey resented her father, who bought her china dolls and kissed her on the forehead at night. Tracey convinced herself that he was two different people. She had met Jekyll, and her mother knew Hyde. Her father also managed to convince her that he was Father Christmas.

As a child, Tracey watched him staggering through the hallway talking gibberish and pointed to him laughing, saying, "The drunken master, what other impressions can you do?" Tracey's mother looked on with a blank expression. More often Tracey's father had spent his week's wages at the pub, and there would be no food in the cupboards. Carol never offered to make him coffee, hoping he would pass out on the kitchen table or sofa until morning.

Carol always had porridge in the cupboards or bubble and squeak on the menu. She had long since had a contingency plan or been able to improvise at a moment's notice. She lived by her wits and foretold calamity by instinct.

Tracey's younger brother Vince saw less of the violence as her father mellowed with age.

Dave idealised Tracey, his little princess. He often bought her expensive gifts and gave her money to lavish on herself. He and Carol lived in a council house they had purchased during the Thatcher years, and the mortgage was now paid off.

Tracey failed to convince herself that her father would ever challenge a decision or choice that she had made. She never wanted to believe he would ever question her decisions based on racial difference. Who was she kidding?

The kitchen door sprang open. Dave said, "Guess who won!" Both Carol and Tracey stared at him.

Tracey raised her chin. "Dad, what did you say to Mum about Tyresse?"

Dave threw his eyes to the ground and walked to the furthest end of the kitchen extension.

"Who is he then?" Dave enquired.

"My friend," Tracey responded.

"Friend!" Dave shouted and pivoted on his heel to face Tracey. All the muscles in his face were flexing.

Tracey stood up, "What's the matter, Dad?"

"How could you ask me that?" Dave said with disdain.

"Well!" Tracey heckled, folding her arms.

"Why did I come back 'ere," Dave mumbled throwing his arms in the air indiscriminately as he steered past Tracey.

"I am talking to you. Dad," Tracey said boldly.

Dave swung round to face Tracey, "Now don't push me too far Tray." Cursing obscenities, he then marched out of the front door.

Tracey could not contain her anguish and clambered upstairs to the bathroom. She thrust her index finger down her throat, contorting her facial muscles as the warm tissue contracted to fold around her finger. She was on her knees and sobbing. The pulling sensation as the hunger pains ensued compounded her pain. Tracey focused on the numbness creeping into her hip from the cold tiled floor and sat against the bath panel.

Downstairs in the kitchen, her mother was speaking frantically on the phone. It was Auntie Lorraine. The voice of reason. Mum always sought to be rescued by Auntie Lorraine, her sister by default of a one-night stand with the neighbour.

Tracey then strolled into the living room and rang Tyresse. "Hi," she said.

"You OK?" asked Tyresse

"Well, that would depend on whether I could wake up in a perfect world," Tracey answered.

"What's up?" Tyresse exhaled.

Tracey stated, "Some of us only like to see ourselves reflected in the mirror." Puzzled, Tyresse asked what she meant. Tracey shook her head, "You won't be getting an invitation for dinner."

"Who's objecting?" he enquired.

"The big bad wolf," she responded.

"Oh," the penny dropped, Tyresse was silent. Tracey felt ashamed; agitated, not knowing what else to say.

"I'll turn him around." Tyresse laughed.

Tracey visualised a knight in shining armour who didn't see the lance about to pierce him in the chest. "Yeah OK," Tracey responded unconvinced.

Why did she bother to say anything? This was new territory, dating a black guy. It was one thing knowing your father was racist, it was another having his views directly impact on your own life.

Tracey was now determined to remain resolute; doing what was right as opposed to what fit. Tracey was compelled to consider the part she played in condoning her father's bigoted view of people from other races, cultures and creeds. She had to admit that she had ignored his prejudices instead of challenging his fears and preconceived ideas about people he knew very little about. She might be considered two-faced, fighting for the cause of racial integration because it suited her current circumstances. Tracey disliked being alienated and frowned upon. She felt betrayed by her own. Mum was OK, but then Mum lived firmly planted on the fence; playing it safe.

Tracey entertained small talk with Tyresse as her mind drifted to the greater task of containing her father's wrath. Why did it have to be so complicated, she wondered.

Hanging up the phone, Tracey contemplated going back to her shared accommodation for peace, away from all this calamity. She did not want to deal with him, to hear him try to justify his thoughts and actions. She clenched her fists against her temples either side and stared up at the ceiling. Tracey knew her mum would be distraught. It would ruin her Christmas.

Tracey laughed. She thought: *Christmas, Christ! The closest this lot got to the essence of Christmas was her father in a red suit, inflatable belly and magazines outlining the TV programmes for the festive season.* He had long since given up the charade; now they just sat; a good excuse for time off work.

Tracey felt sad. She and Vince had grown up, and neither of them had children yet. She smiled when she thought about Tyresse's family all together singing carols celebrating Christ's birth at midnight on Christmas Eve night. Tyresse explained what Christmas signified. The birth of the Christ child born to die that sinners can be saved and inherit eternal life.

Dusk had long since passed, and the curtains were still open. Tracey fell asleep on the sofa, nestled in a quilt while watching TV.

26.

At the station, Tia pressed the phone against her ear, straining to hear Xavier on the phone. Tia ascertained that he was still at his parent's home but wanted to leave. She had seen pictures of his holiday home in the picturesque Hampshire woodlands and wondered why he would want to leave.

Tia thought he was selfish and ungrateful for not appreciating his family and privileged background and told him so. Xavier laughed, saying, "Walk in my shoes."

Tia did not hesitate to respond, "Sure, hand them over."

The train pulled into the station and Xavier responded saying "They're too big for you to fill Tia."

"So, when am I going to see you?" said Tia hurriedly

"Probably next week."

She hung up the phone and looked across the tracks as the train pulled out of the station, bound for Upminster.

Tia had arrived home late last night for the holidays and was out visiting friends this morning.

Later in the afternoon, Tia intended to confront her mother, Faye, about her birth father. Why hadn't she told her about him? The only thing her mother had admitted was that he was a black man who she'd had a brief relationship with as a teenager. Her mother also told her that her family had threatened to abandon her if she did not have her adopted at birth.

In those days, single mothers and children of mixed heritage in their community were considered taboo. Faye had been encouraged to give her baby away. However, she had refused. Tia's father had bowed under the pressure and disappeared for good; never to be seen again.

Faye fought to keep Tia at the cost of losing her family. They abandoned her. Faye had moved into a council flat and began raising Tia on her own.

Bob got together with Mum when Tia was a small child. Tia doesn't remember when, as he had always been in her life for as far back as she could remember. Her school friends loved her for who she was, not what she was. It was never an issue. Deep down Tia knew she was different but never questioned or voiced whether Bob was her father. Faye just reaffirmed that Bob was her father and dismissed her curiosity.

A year later, in-depth discussions about reproduction during a biology lesson confirmed Tia's deepest fears, eliminating Bob as her biological father. Although she had been told this, her heart did not want to believe it. She wanted to talk to her parents about this. However, she never found the courage to confront the truth; to know why her difference was never celebrated, acknowledged and appreciated. She felt like a dirty secret.

Tia was of the impression her difference wasn't significant, that it made no difference to find out. She began to believe perhaps there wasn't a need to make too much of a fuss about her birth father. She had a family who knew her for whatever she was. Tia suppressed her enquiring mind by preoccupying herself with a string of meaningless relationships looking for love, adoration and acceptance.

Tia had arrived at her destination and left the platform. She scanned her local high street. It felt different, although nothing had changed but her presence. It had been some time since she had been here. Living in Pimlico was a far cry from East London. The monumental buildings which shaped the landscape of central London compared with the defaced shop fronts for short-term lease present in the Essex High Street had formed a profound impression upon Tia. She never imagined that it would matter. Being exposed to talented students who cultivated an ethos of excellence had raised her aspirations and expectations of herself. Tia was learning to trust in herself; to believe in her own convictions. Tia was beginning to recognise that this would take time as she had been conditioned to think with a hive mind.

Her mind drifted to Xavier. She lusted after him but felt nothing in the act of lovemaking. The excitement was in the chase; being wooed. Once captured, the thrill had ceased. Tia smiled, savouring the essence of the games; some old behaviours were hard to change. Men admired her form, her beauty and this pleased her.

Tia met her mother at the mall. They ordered coffee and sat to face one another. Tia's mother broke the silence in her attempt to gain an advantage, "It's nice to have you for the holidays, T."

"Yeah, it's nice to be home," Tia lied.

Faye said, "We've bought presents for everyone."

Tia was not excited by this as she always received inferior presents to her siblings, who were Bob's birth children. Tia hated this pretence. She felt as if she had taken the blue pill; a bite of the forbidden apple and could see all things, feeling the pain of the reality of her situation. She did not feel as though she had been shielded from the truth but denied the right to establish her own identity.

Truthingdom

Tia could no longer contain herself, "Mum who is my dad?"

Faye flushed in the face, began fidgeting in her chair and stammered her response. "What does it matter, Tia? That was so long ago, in the past,"

Tia wasted no time in keeping up the momentum, "Mum this man is my father; I deserve to know the truth."

The restaurant fell silent, all eyes were diverted to their table; however, no one dared look them directly in the face. Tia looked around; instinctively all eyes then shifted elsewhere. Faye's breathing was shallow, her bowed chin almost touching her chest. "Tia, keep your voice down," Faye pleaded.

Tia took a deep breath and continued to explain, "I was too black to fit in with the white girls and too white to fit in with the black girls and too naive to challenge you further as a little girl about who I was. You shut me down, and I don't know how to handle the situation." Tia was now trembling, "Or how to fight for the right to know the truth." Tia was now leaning forward over the table, "Tell me now, who my dad is?"

Faye raised her head, "He was some guy who I'd seen a couple of times, had a night of passion with and got pregnant." Tia was deflated, expecting more. Tia asked her mother if she knew his name. "Carl Peters," Faye stated emphatically. "That's all I know."

"Where did he come from Mum," Tia pressed.

"Peckham," Faye answered under her breath, insisting she did not know more than that.

Tia sat back, relieved to know more. She caught the eyes of a woman staring straight at her. "Would you like to know more?" Widening her eyes, the lady sitting on the next table apologised profusely. Tia looked away and focused her attention on her mother who had raised her hand to shield her face in embarrassment.

Tia and her mother did some more Christmas shopping before going home. *Carl Peters:* Tia thought. She tried to imagine what he looked like. She resembled her mother, but who knows, she may well look like her dad. She peered into shop windows as they walked by, trying to catch a glimpse of herself to see if there was something about her own reflection that she did not recognise. *Silly:* she thought.

Tia wasn't really listening to her mother as they walked around the mall. She was thinking about how she could contact her father. Tia thought of the telephone directory, but most people were ex-directory now. She could consider searching the births and deaths records in Essex, providing he was born there.

"Tia, I am talking to you," Faye was tugging at her jacket.

"Yes, Mum," looking over at her mother. Faye proceeded to talk about everything but the revelation of her life. Tia laughed; mumbling to herself, "She really doesn't get it."

Trailing behind her mum, Tia called Tracey and told her about her dad. Tia caught herself talking about him as if he was already in her life. *Needy* :she thought.

Tracey was stunned and began asking Tia lots of questions that she could not answer.

27.

Aarti landed at Muzaffarpur Airport in the late afternoon. She collected her luggage from the baggage carousel and headed for the arrivals foyer. For a moment she had forgotten her torment and developed a spring in her step. The sliding doors parted, and she stepped out into the moist atmosphere. The penetrating sun massaged her skin, and the warm breeze danced through her hair. Aarti twisted her neck to and fro in time to the rhythm of the wind.

"Beti," Aarti recognised her father's voice approaching. He apologised for being late and explained that Aarti's mother was at home preparing for her arrival.

Aarti leaned out of the car window; closing her eyes, allowing the wind to rush past her face. A bicycle veered in front of Vishnu's vehicle.

The man then began shouting, "Mind where you are going," whilst hitting his loud old brass bell. Aarti looked back.

Her father was shouting back at the man. "No, you are blind!" waving his hands about.

Aarti looked at her father laughing and said, "Are we home soon?"

"Yes," her father said, "You are home."

Aarti laid her head back and felt her shoulders relax as the humid air caressed her. The truck bobbed up and down along the terracotta dirt coloured road and blew dust up into a whirlwind when Vishnu slowed and sped up on the meandering roads to

Durgapur. In the far distance, they were chasing the glowing yellow-orange sunset. Flexing her nostrils as they passed through the villages, she could smell warm spiced milk, ginger and masala curry. She closed her eyes again in an effort to capture the sights, sounds and smells of the region. She could hear the cowbell; looking out she spotted the silky brown coat of the enormous creature slowly sauntering alongside the truck, flickering its ears. She tried to imagine a cow walking alongside a bus in London and smiled.

Aarti's father began to talk about a welfare rally he had recently been involved in and raised 52,000 rupees. Aarti glanced over at her father who was engrossed in what he was saying whilst driving up the dual carriageway. Aarti focused on the black and white roadblocks which defined the roads and compared the vista presented to the monumental order of British streets.

The vehicle slowed down; they had arrived. Vishnu blew his horn several times, and the gateman ran across the courtyard to unlock the gate. Aarti looked up at the old farmhouse. It was dusk, and the soft lighting of the external wall lamps illuminated the entrance with a soft shade of tangerine, which reflected off the walls of the old stone house.

Aarti's mother ran out onto the veranda with outstretched arms, her long white scarf blustering in the wind behind her. Aarti began sobbing as she leapt out of the jeep and ran to greet her mother. Aarti and her mother's words were leaping over one another to be heard. The two of them were now locked in an intimate embrace and rocking from side to side whilst Vishnu prompted the house help to collect Aarti's bags from the car.

Vishnu now steered Aarti and her mother into the house. Aarti did not realise how much she missed her parents and her mother country.

Aarti's mother's hands were waving in the air as she tripped over her words. She was trying to explain the itinerary for Aarti's stay, beginning with a pre-wedding celebration that evening. "Ah, not yours," her mother quickly interjecting, "Your cousin, Aunty Bhagwati's daughter Prema; they are so looking forward to you coming."

Aarti's mother was now standing. "Look," she said, as she hurried over to a desk in the corner and pulled out a folder. She rushed back to Aarti's side. She then paused, took a deep breath and thrust a photo of Aarti's betrothed in front of her. Aarti sat waiting for the words to catch up, lifting her bottom lip and clasping her mouth shut.

"He is handsome," Aarti whispered.

"Yes, only the best for our daughter," her mother said proudly. "He is going to be at the party tonight," her mother said. "His parents are going to be there too," Aarti's mother said excitedly. Aarti sat quietly, staring in front of her. Her father stood close by listening but dared not interrupt. "Oh," her mother said, "I have made three outfits for you, I hope you like them." Aarti's eyes were now cast down; she was tired. Her mother then said, "You look tired, maybe you should have some rest." She continued, "I have aired your room."

Aarti made her way up the stairs, opened her bedroom door and looked around the room. Nothing had been moved; her photos, maps, books and trinkets were as she had left them. She walked over to the window and leaned out looking into the courtyard below. The cool breeze stroked her face. She could smell roasted corn and warm turmeric milk. She was home. She lay on her bed, listening to the wind chimes on her verandah, and fell fast asleep.

Aarti's mother called out to her as she walked into the bedroom, "Wake up Aarti, it's time to get ready." Her mother was carrying two beautifully woven outfits for Aarti to try on. Aarti roused from sleep and stretched her body.

Aarti chose to wear the cream lace and satin salwar kameez, which hugged her figure like a glove, with a matching chiffon scarf that sat just off her sparkle dusted shoulders. She wore her hair in a bouffant held together by a wide-toothed, diamond-studded decorative comb. Her mother strategically placed tiny cream flowers in her hair. Aarti's pink lips shimmered like a liquid mirror, and her cheeks were slightly flushed pink.

Aarti walked out into the courtyard. It was the cool of the evening. The light from the porch flickered against her flawless complexion. Vishnu held his chest and stood in awe of her beauty. "Beti, you are like the stars at night, beautiful and bright." Aarti smiled, rubbing her cheek gently against his.

When they arrived, the party was buzzing with excitement. It was formal dress. Prema's family were privileged. Her father was a banker, and Aarti was aware that those who were invited were from the higher echelons of society. It felt more like a piranha's swimming pool.

Prema was covered in precious jewels and holding a glass of champagne. She came rushing over to Aarti and greeted her. "It's so good to see you" she continued, "How's London?"

"Oh, it's good thanks," Aarti gripped her tongue.

"He's here you know," Prema threw her gaze over Aarti shoulder. Aarti froze, her body stiffened. Aarti's mother rushed over and held her arm, spinning her around gently. Aarti's father followed, standing close by.

Aarti could feel the butterflies in her stomach; she felt clammy, then cold. Aarti looked up and focused on her intended. She was pleasantly surprised. He was indeed handsome and gazing back at her. He bowed slightly and stood back exposing both his parents who were also looking at her. Aarti smiled and greeted them, stooping somewhat as a mark of respect. His parents stood quietly whilst the others buzzed around them. They were civil and exercised good manners. She could not fault them. Aarti felt as though she was just going through the motions. She was unable to focus. Her mind drifted back to recent events.

"You look beautiful," Ajay whispered.

"Oh, thank you," Aarti said lowering her head. She felt shy. Why? She was slightly annoyed. Perhaps it was the whole situation and intentions of both parents.

Ajay, her betrothed, was polite and appeared relaxed, nonetheless eager to be acquainted with Aarti. At times Aarti was able to engage in conversation, at other times she was distracted by her own thoughts. Prema flittered back and forth. She had learnt the art of engaging effectively to achieve her own ends. Prema made every effort to familiarise herself with the goings on in Aarti's group. Aarti wondered how she had time to enjoy her own engagement party.

Ajay's parents were financially secure and had a large townhouse. The scene was set, and Aarti only had to say yes. It all seemed so simple. She wasn't in love but how much did that have to do with it. He seemed pleasant enough; was that enough? Aarti was unsure what to think. The in-laws were becoming acquainted whilst she and Ajay stood aimlessly, trying to hear the tail end of other people's conversations.

Aarti sighed. "How is your evening so far?" Ajay said raising his voice.

"It's fine thank you," she said hesitantly. Aarti looked around as if wanting to be rescued but there was no escape.

"You look lovely tonight," Ajay now appeared nervous, tapping the side of his glass.

"Thank you," Aarti answered, clasping her left hand behind her back, staring over his shoulder.

Ajay beckoned, "Would you like another drink?"

"No thank you," Aarti replied. Aarti's forehead felt moist, as did her nose. She felt flustered. She reached for the fan in her bag and began fanning herself. The crest of dew on her face now felt cool.

Ajay asked more impatiently, "Are you sure you do not want something to drink?"

"No, I'm all right, excuse me," Aarti said brushing past him. She shuffled quickly down the hallway towards the lavatory and pressed her back against the door behind her. The toilet looked more like a personal en-suite. She observed the black marble surfaces, oval mirrors, fresh flowers and scented hand cream. Gazing into the mirror, she saw the pained expression watching her blink. She wondered whether to convince her reflection to flee or face the music whatever the dance. She snapped out of her daydream and headed back down the hallway.

Ajay was a promising student at the Central University of Rajasthan studying chemical sciences. He wanted to manipulate gases in order to produce clean air to rid big cities of air pollution. His mother described him as polite and sensitive. She was extremely proud of him. She had great expectations of him and was mindful of those contemplating marriage.

"So, how long will you be in London?" Ajay's mother asked Aarti.

"One year," Aarti answered. Ajay's mother dropped her eyes slowly to study her attire. Aarti looked down awkwardly stroking the front of her outfit, then glanced up again. Ajay's mother was looking at her with a fixed expression.

"There you are," Ajay sounded out of breath. "I was looking everywhere for you."

Aarti smiled; relieved she said, "I would like a glass of fruit punch now please." Ajay hurried off and returned with a full glass of pink cocktail.

Ajay's mother began fanning herself vigorously and blowing "I feel faint," she said. Ajay stepped forward to girdle her from the side and led her out of the side door towards the terrace.

Shortly afterwards, he returned. He was very apologetic. He had arranged for transport to take his parents home as his mother was poorly.

Aarti and Prema walked them out to the car and watched as they drove away. "You're probably getting too close to her panda bear," Prema chuckled.

"What do you mean?" Aarti questioned,

"That is what you are here for, isn't it?" Prema widened her eyes, folded her arms and walked back inside.

Aarti slept until mid-morning the next day. Her mother was chattering to her neighbour in the kitchen whilst starting preparations for the evening meal. Aarti asked what they were having for lunch. Her mother declared, "Soup with puri's." Aarti observed her mother dipping the spatula into the hot oil and scooping the warm cooked golden disks floating on the top. Her mother talked about her secret soup recipe, adding lemongrass and grated nutmeg. She would not, however, share how this meal was prepared. Aarti looked on as her mother repeatedly crushed garlic and ginger with her stone pestle and mortar.

Her mother spoke about dinner as if she was telling a love story. She held her fingertips to her nose as if smelling the bouquet of fragrances as she described; turmeric as the yellow coloured sands of mustard on your pallet; saffron, the fine wispy threads of rose like orange, sweet floral aroma; being mesmerised by the captivating tang of ginger's sharp and potent, mouth-watering sensation. Her mother did not need any help in the kitchen. Her mother was able to express her creativity through food.

Aarti slipped away and strolled into the back garden. The air was scented with the sweet woody scent of the Kadam flower; blending with the moistened chlorophyll which was ever present in the atmosphere.

Aarti sat under the age-old khejari tree, where she had carved out her name as a child and sipped on chilled homemade Lassi. Aarti tossed her head back and assumed the lotus position. Slowly she brought her head forward, positioning her fontanelle in exact alignment with the sun's rays which beamed down on through to the soles of her upturned feet, while the fresh breeze blew gently through her long mane. She tried to clear her mind; to relax whilst attempting to induce a state of serenity. To be still, motionless, hearing the sounds of the wind, the crickets and the branches singing in the wind. Aarti's body felt limp. She felt her body drifting away.

28.

Aarti's mother was chatting on the phone. Aarti strolled past her and sat outside on a wicker chair on the patio. A few days had since passed, and Aarti was savouring the remaining time before she returned to Britain.

Aarti had been to the temple early that morning at dawn. She felt incongruent, observing others around her consumed with their own thoughts. Aarti blessed the offering of fruit and lit a candle. She sat and watched as the wick was overwhelmed by the flame, symbolising the dampening of her own ego, while gazing at the fire which burnt upwards denoting increased knowledge and understanding.

Having been exposed to another culture, another existence, Aarti found herself dissecting ancient ritualistic practices, critiquing the processes rather than just being wholeheartedly absorbed in them. She deeply inhaled the strong scent of melted ghee close by. The melted butter fat released a dark smoke which swirled up towards the richly patterned tiled ceiling. The surrounds were lavishly decorated in bright, vivacious colours. Dyed linen fabrics were pinned to the walls. The air was filled with the murmurs of people chanting and praying. The intense spicy, woody, earthy scents of sandalwood enveloped her surrounds.

Aarti was mesmerised by the slower pace of life in India, a stark comparison to the hustle and bustle of London. She was thankful to have the mental space to reflect on past events and consider how best to move on and continue living her life to the full.

Later that day she sat at the main family dining table which was placed in the expansive lounge with its high ceilings and monumental pillars. The old farmhouse was built in the late 1900's. Her parents had renovated the derelict building, which now stood like a grand old relic of its former self.

She sat on a lounger watching her mother gather flowers in the garden through the French style patio doors, which were wide open. A cool fresh breeze filled the space and Aarti threw off her sandals and raised her neck. *That was refreshing: she* thought.

Aarti had never questioned her beliefs. Faith was a far cry from the methodology of deduction and enquiry applied at University. Something had changed. Her faith was steadfast. However, her outlook on life had changed. No longer did she see through a shrouded veil. She could now see the adulterated perspectives of life filtered amongst the purity and untainted fragments of humanity and spirit. She had grown up, finally, a woman forged by her own adversity and torment.

Aarti was heartbroken having imagined a fantastic portrayal of a picturesque life in a far away never-never land, full of hope and promise. Betrayed by the carnivorous lust of a depraved mind, her dreams were shattered, annihilated, destroyed utterly. Aarti gasped, silencing her outcry. She pressed the palm of her hand on her pulsating sternum and cried bitterly, bowing her head to avoid detection.

It was three o'clock. It was hot and hazy. Music sifted through the upstairs corridors. The classical art of Jalyantra meandered its way across the bedroom like rippling waves. The melodic octaves danced in one chorus, floating in her mind. Aarti opened her eyes as if emerging from paradise and stared at the array of luminous flowers clasped within a beautifully decorated vase stained luscious cobalt blue. For a time, she had snatched a moment of peace. She lay still.

"Aarti," her mother called. "Wake up, it's time to get ready,"

Aarti stirred and leaned on her elbow. "Where are we going?"

"Prema's parents are having guests this afternoon. Ah, and Ajay will be there," her mother chuckled. Aarti sighed gently, thinking the itinerary to be relentless.

Aarti had lost all sense of time. The days seemed to roll into one another. Aarti was caught up in her own thoughts. Harsh realities were painful. She felt shackled and imprisoned in those memories and feelings.

It was a grand affair. Aarti observed Prema gliding effortlessly from clique to clique. Aarti watched as her mother bustled past a gentleman, knocking his toupee slightly off centre. He straightened his back, twitched his face and tossed his head a little in an effort to reposition it. Aarti sniggered, and Ajay stepped forward into view. Aarti pulled her cup away from her face and spilt red fruit punch over Ajay's cream suit. Aarti threw her hand over her gaping mouth. Everything was happening in slow motion. As Aarti reached out, Prema grabbed Ajay's arm and whisked him away into the vast hallway. Aarti followed.

"What happened?" Prema asked,

"It was an accident," Aarti replied,

"What did I say that upset you?" Ajay asked.

"Nothing, it wasn't you," Aarti said. Ajay handed his jacket to a housemaid. Prema and Ajay looked baffled. "Sorry, OK?" Aarti persisted.

"How long are you here for?" Ajay asked.

Aarti replied, "Another week." They stared awkwardly at one another.

Prema added, "Well we will have to organise something."

"Already have," Aunt Bhagwati interjected. Aarti looked across at the tag team circling.

Ajay grinned slightly at Aunt Bhagwati. Aarti felt like the ball that had just been snookered. Prema gently manoeuvred Aarti back to her mother and glided off in another direction. Aarti looked around her; she wondered if she had missed something. Everything had spiralled so quickly.

"I have not seen *you* before," A lonely voice came from the open doorway. Aarti looked behind her and saw a tall, handsome gentleman smiling at her. Aarti thought him too confident and full of himself. She turned away without replying. "Observing you, I thought you had brains to match your beauty, I never assumed that you were ignorant" He continued, "Yes I assumed too much." Aarti was tempted but did not turn around again.

Ajay returned somewhat flustered. He had gone back to the hotel and changed. His parents were sitting talking to Aunt Bhagwati in one corner of the room. Aarti pointed to two buttons which were not fastened properly. Ajay swung round and adjusted his clothes. Aarti laughed quietly, and Prema offered Ajay a drink to steady his nerves. Ajay gratefully accepted.

Aunt Bhagwati glided in and took Ajay's glass, gave it to his mother and whisked him out to the dance floor. Prema gently gripped Aarti's hand and led her to the dance floor. Ajay joined in the Gair folk dance, rotating and hitting his sticks in rhythm to the percussive music.

Aarti began to sing, she gently tossed her hips repeatedly from side to side and clapped her hands in the air. She danced round in a circle, and Prema threw her hands in the air, her fingers began to dance forming purposeful shapes and movement in time to the drumbeat of the dhol. Aarti was caught up in the rapture of the melody. She began spinning; pivoting on her feet, springboarding off the ground beneath her.

Aarti looked across at her father Vishnu, who was sitting watching the dancers. He sucked on the end of his fingers savouring the flavours of the sweet, smoky chargrilled vegetables served with a variety of chutney sauces.

Aarti collapsed into a chair near the open doorways so that she could still see the dancers on the lawn.

A man stepped into the room and Prema strolled over to him. Aarti cast her eyes across at them. It was Prema's fiancée. She recognised his voice; however, she had been unable to see his features clearly outside of the open doorway earlier that evening. He appeared agitated as he spoke briefly to Prema and moved away. Prema walked briskly across to Aarti. Aarti held Prema's arm.

"We haven't been introduced," Prema's fiancée was standing in front of them. Prema looked across at Veer who was staring wide-eyed at Aarti with a smug smile on his face. "You do not have a drink, what can I get you?" Veer asked. Prema glared at Veer, who remained fixated on Aarti.

Prema excused herself and hurried out onto the balcony. Aarti followed her. Prema was crying. "What's wrong Prema?" Aarti asked. "We are to be married shortly...I am just happy, that's all."

Aarti agreed to stay overnight with Prema. Her aunt made hot cinnamon tea and bid them a good night's rest. Aarti woke up during the early hours and observed Prema out on the verandah. Aarti's warm feet pressed on the cool tiles underneath her as she walked towards Prema. There was a gentle breeze. It was the dead of night; only the crickets sang out. She called out to Prema, and she looked up. Prema smiled at Aarti and patted the velvet cushion next to her.

Aarti crept slowly towards Prema. Prema explained that her parents thought they were the perfect match. Aarti, however, was not convinced that Prema's fiancée was agreeable with the match.

Although Aarti rebuked herself for being unsure whether Prema's fiancée was the man for her cousin. His advances towards her and his disregard of her cousin during the party set Aarti on her guard. Aarti questioned his intentions. "Prema are you sure he is the right one for you? He seems boastful."

"Are you judging him? You don't even know him," Prema responded angrily. "You travelled to London, and you think that makes you better than everyone else!"

Aarti thought Prema's response clichéd. Nonetheless, Aarti thought herself clumsy to have even said what she did. Prema was sensitive and in love. Aarti was now standing, gripping her hands together. She pleaded with Prema to forgive her. Pouting, Prema lowered her head and began crying. She said, "I am 25 years old; yes, my family has money, but time waits for no man, my childbearing years are fleeing. You are 19, beautiful and studying in England." Aarti saw the pain in her eyes, the fear of lost opportunity if she did not cling to the life raft. Prema now spoke in a whisper. "Veer's parents are rich. My parents wanted the best for me, for my children." Aarti knelt down beside her and began stroking Prema's hair gently. Prema rested her head on Aarti's shoulder. Aarti stared up at the moon. The moon seemed larger than life. Its light was radiant against the indigo sky, and the stars were numerous across the expanse of infinite space.

29.

Xavier pulled the silver needle slowly out of his arm; crimson coloured liquid oozed out of his veins, forming tributaries which flowed with gravity. Xavier pressed a cloth on his arm to stop the bleeding. He took a deep breath and swayed as his head spun round and round. This was good stuff, he thought, as he had not had a good a high for months. He chuckled and shouted out, "Woh!" He began laughing out loud. Dark shadows danced on the walls. He pointed out to them, stabbing at them with his finger in the dark. He felt a warm sensation travelling through his body. He was fearless, unyielding against those who challenged or even questioned him.

The door knocked. Xavier rolled onto his stomach. "Hold on" he shouted.

Tia stood in the doorway. "So, you came home early then," she said, brushing past him, letting herself in. "I brought some bubbly for later," Xavier did not respond. He sat on a chair and slung his feet up onto the chair opposite. "Did you miss me then?" Tia asked.

Xavier turned slowly to look at Tia and asked, "What can I do for you?"

Tia replied, "More like what I can do for you!"

Xavier laughed to himself, got up and crawled back into bed.

Xavier smiled to himself as Tia pressed against him. She did not realise that Xavier resented her. Xavier saw Tia as a whore. Tia smiled, thinking that she was pleasing him and exerting her dominance, taking him when she wanted. Neither of them was victorious. Both of them were degrading themselves according to their own warped reasoning.

Tia woke up. It was late, and Xavier was nowhere to be found. It was cold. The flat was in darkness. She flicked the light switches. Nothing worked. She assumed he had gone out to top up the electric card. Four hours later he still had not come back and was not answering his phone. Tia stood smoking in the lit hallway outside the flat door and began to curse. She was angry he had left her on her own with no electricity. Even the bubbly had gone.

Xavier was miles away, drinking at a local wine bar with Tyresse. He had met Tyresse at home and brought the bottle of bubbly to fire up the evening before they set off. Xavier admired Tyresse's charisma and enjoyed watching the power and control he had over the opposite sex.

"Someone is looking for you," Tyresse said pushing his phone across to Xavier.

"Please," Xavier responded uninterested.

Tia read Tyresse's response; WE'RE AT MOUNTFIELD'S HAVING A DRINK COME AND JOIN US. Tia rang Tracey in a flood of tears. Tracey tried to console her and drove to meet her at a local night spot.

Sputtering Tia said, "Tray, all my life I have loved and cared for everyone else and all people do is hurt me."

"Right, what you going to do about it?" Tracey said indignantly, "When does it stop?" Tia's mascara ran down her cheeks. Tia did not have an answer. Tracey raised her voice, "Tia, look at me." Tia looked up slowly and raised her hands to cover her face, bearing superficial keloid scars running on the insides of her wrists like dislodged train tracks. Tracey threw her body back and pressed her lips close together. "Tia, what do you want to do?" Tracey whispered. Tia shook her head maladroitly. Tracey took a deep breath, braced herself and said, "Tia, did you want to go and meet them?" Tia looked up at Tracey like a wounded lion. Tracey then said, "What are you looking at me like that for?"

Tia then stood up and said, "What kind of friend would…"

Tracey interjected, "What kind of friend would what? What? You don't need me to cause you pain, you are doing well enough on your own, and then you want me to join you in your misery." Tracey was now standing. They alerted others around them, who began to watch. No one moved; they just looked on. Tia walked out. Tracey descended like a bag of lead, throwing herself into the chair.

Tracey had mixed feelings. She felt sympathy and anger stirred together. The old technicolour film played over and over in her mind. She fought past memories of oppression and entrapment which embraced her. Filled with regret she stormed out to find Tia.

Tia was sitting in a bus shelter. Tracey sat alongside her. Tracey then asked, "What are you going to do?"

Tia threw her arms forward, "Tray, I just turned up at his place. I wasn't invited."

Tracey interjected, "So, what's your point?" Tia noted Tracey's protest and took a deep breath. Tracey then said, "No one has a right to treat you like trash," Tracey's voice now raised," You deserve respect; you are somebody. He is treating you worse than an animal; at least an animal is left food and water in a bowl." Tracey pulled back her tongue and twisted her mouth in an effort to keep her tongue inside.

Tia was crying out loud, pacing up and down and grabbing at her midriff. Tracey leapt up and pulled Tia towards her and squeezed her tight. Tia began heaving and choking. Tracey stepped back and patted Tia's back. Tia knelt down. Tracey then pulled her away from the vomit which spread across the pavement in front of her. Tia was flushed pink; saliva dripping from the side of her mouth. Tracey dragged Tia to stand and sat her down on the bench. The night light in the bus stop highlighted her contorted face. Tracey looked closely at her porous skin, smoothed over with caramel mousse.

Tracey began shouting, "Pull yourself together T!" She repeated herself several times. Tia felt stifled with heat, ripping her scarf away from her neck. Tracey then unzipped Tia's puffer jacket; exposing the beads of sweat on Tia's chest and forehead.

Tia fell silent. Her shoulders rhythmically moving up and down. Sucking air in and out as rich puffs of smoke rose from her nostrils, while her eyes remained fixated on the ground beneath her. Tracey tossed her head away from the stench of regurgitated pulp pieces splattered on the ground.

Tracey was now gripped with emotion and fought back the tears. Tia began groaning, her bottom jaw hanging. Tracey stood in front of her and wrapped her arms around her. Tracey threw her head back and screamed out; however, no sound rang out. Tracey was now filled with pity. Tia's sorrow touched her soul. She felt their hearts ache in unison, knowing that they were sharing the same pain. Tracey wept, "I am sorry Tia, I am sorry they hurt you." Tia groaned repeatedly. Tracey began to shake on the spot. She was desperate to regain composure. She felt vulnerable. Tia lay on Tracey's chest, gripping her arm as if stopping herself from falling. Tia felt out of her senses, cold and numb. Hot and nauseous.

Tia's shirt was torn, ripped from the neckline. Tia sat still while Tracey zipped her jacket and pulled her hoody over her dishevelled hair. Tracey sucked in her stomach to stop from toppling, cupped Tia over the shoulder and pulled her away from the bench. Tia moved voluntarily, stumbling forward, placing one foot in front of the other.

30.

Tracey turned the key gently and crept up the stairs. "Oh, you decided to come home then," her dad said standing with a cup of tea in the kitchen doorway.

Tracey explained that she and some friends stayed out late last night and didn't get in until really late. It was Christmas Eve, and Mum was baking.

Vince was in the lounge watching TV with his girlfriend. Tracey greeted them and joined her mother in the kitchen. Dave disappeared into the lounge. Tracey thought he probably felt safer in numbers, considering their vexation the other day.

Tracey drank more coffee to ease the pain in her stomach. She hadn't eaten since lunchtime the day before. She thought her face looked puffy, but she wasn't sure. Her mother offered to make her a sandwich, but she refused. Tracey told her mother that she had eaten breakfast.

"Aunty Lorraine is coming to help prepare for Christmas dinner later," Carol said.

Tracey liked Aunt Lorraine as she spoke her mind. "Nice! Is she bringing her new man with her?"

"No, she's bringing Trina; you haven't met her," Carol stated, raising her eyebrows.

"What about Trina?" Tracey said hesitantly. Carol's eyes widened and her lips curved to the side. "Mum, what you saying?" Tracey pressed, tilting forward.

"She's your aunt's FRIEND," Carol replied.

"Yeah, like?" Tracey began saying before being interrupted by Vince who meandered into the kitchen. "How's life treating you, Vinny? You still in love?" Tracey asked.

"Yeah, Yeah," Vincent answered. "You?"

Tracey looked across at her mother. "Yeah, I am good."

"Seeing anyone?" Vincent asked casually.

"No, just enjoying life," Tracey answered.

Carol raised an eyebrow and folded her arms, thinking: *What a coward and a hypocrite.*

The dinner table was set. Dave, his best friend and his wife, were sitting in the lounge drinking beer and eggnog. Tracey was helping Mum put the finishing touches to the dinner table. Aunt Lorraine gave her apologies for not coming earlier, arriving at 7pm on the dot.

Tracey opened the door. Her aunt stepped in and greeted her with a hug, smothering Tracey with her fur collar and sweet perfume. Lorraine then stepped back.

"Meet Trina," Aunt Lorraine said in a high-pitched voice.

"Hi," Tracey said in a reserved lower voice. Trina stepped forward and smiled, bowing her head slightly. She looked like a Russian bombshell. She stretched her hand towards Tracey. Tracey studied her elongated face and perfect symmetry. The light reflected off her light green coloured corneas, set against her smooth, bright complexion and pearl fuchsia pink thin lips. Tracey was impressed, "Nice lip colour," Tracey smiled.

Trina smiled back bowing her head again, "Nice to meet you,"

Dave lunged forward and grabbed her coat. Trina released her grip and smiled lowering her eyes. "Dad, you can put your tongue away now," Tracey whispered under her breath. Dave flung Trina's coat over the stair bannister in the hallway and rushed back in to pull a chair out for her at the dinner table. Avoiding Dave; Carol swung her arms to the left with the gravy boat to evade spilling it over Vincent who had already sat down at the table.

"Would you like a drink?" Dave asked.

"A gin and tonic please," Trina replied.

Dave rushed into the lounge.

"Would anyone else like a drink?" Carol asked apologetically.

Dave's best friend's wife, Sarah gave Carol a stern look, "Brandy and coke please."

Barry who was Dave's best friend stood up, "I'll get it, Carol, you carry on." Barry murmured to Dave, "What you playing at?"

Dave was busy mixing drinks. "What?" Dave looked up.

"Stop wagging your tail, mate" Barry implored.

"She is a cracker, isn't she," Dave said excitedly. He then pushed past Barry and headed for the dinner table set up in the fairly large extension attached to the kitchen.

Barry returned to the table. Sarah was annoyed, staring at Dave across the table. Dave had been drinking. The smell of fermented malt and grain, the bitter, sweet, nutty odour filled the air around his person.

Dave sat glaring at Trina.

"Dad close ya mouth and pass me the potatoes," Tracey was annoyed. Sarah was mortified.

Tracey observed Vincent leaning over towards his girlfriend, whispering in her ear and biting her earlobe. Turning to Barry she overheard him whisper to his wife Sarah through slightly parted lips, "We just sat down; stop it, dessert hasn't been served yet." Tracey rolled her eyes.

"Would you like some more gravy Tray," Carol held the gravy boat over her plate.

"No thanks Mum," Tracey replied. Carol then shifted to the next guest, then the next, until everyone had been offered gravy.

Dave stood up raising his glass, "Let us drink to glad tidings and beautiful women."

In a raised voice Lorraine said, "Yes indeed," and passionately kissed Trina full on the mouth. Dave toppled down onto his chair stunned into silence.

Instantly enraged he staggered off his chair and slapped Lorraine in the face. Lorraine jumped up, grabbed her plate and slung it at him. She then dived forward and began throwing punches at his head. Dave was now stumbling backwards. Vincent grabbed his aunt from behind, and Sarah was shouting, "What the hell is going on here, I've had enough of this, Barry let's go right now."

Carol exasperated, hands Sarah her coat. "Dad what the fuck do you think you are doing; you've lost it," Tracey was furious.

"What do you mean Tray; did you see what just happened?" Vincent was short of breath, coming to his father's defence.

"Shut the fuck up Vincent! He's only mad because Trina wouldn't stroke him," Tracey unrelenting, "He couldn't give a shit if she's a lesbian. Don't you get it, Vince?" Tracey concluded looking at her father spaced out on the kitchen floor.

Trina appeared shaken, standing rigid on the spot. Carol looked downcast as she knelt down to pick up the cutlery and chinaware which lay scattered all over the floor.

"I told you I didn't want to come here tonight," Lorraine shrieked. "Why do you put up with him?"

Carol began weeping silently, too embarrassed to look up at Lorraine. "What do you want me to say?" Carol muttered, "What do you want me to do?"

"What do *you* want to do?" Lorraine shrieked. She was now standing over Carol.

"Tell me what I should do, I am tired and fed up; I just want peace and quiet." Carol was now looking up at Lorraine.

Lorraine knelt down, "Stand up for yourself Carol. What do you need Carol?"

Carol looked around her. Everyone had left the kitchen except Tracey, who stood in the doorway.

"I don't know; to tell you the truth, I am scared," Carol whispered, "I've never had to make decisions as Dave always knows what to do." Lorraine looked across at Tracey.

Tracey stepped forward. "It's OK, Mum; get ready for bed; I'll clean this up."

Vince and his partner had already gone to bed, and Tracey helped her father onto the settee in the lounge. Tracey then took a deep breath and thought about her own selfish reasons why she wanted the institution of marriage to remain intact. Divorce, another statistic; a child from a broken home.

Lorraine put the kettle on, and Trina sat carefully on the edge of a kitchen chair to avoid making any noise or drawing further attention to herself. Lorraine looked across at Tracey and tossed her eyes down on the floor at Carol. Tracey strolled across to her mother. "Come on Mum, sit down," Tracey said gently. Carol stood up, reached for a chair and sat, clenching broken crockery.

"Carol, what's for Christmas Dinner?" Lorraine asked.

Carol looked up wearing a strained smiled on her face. "I got a large turkey from the butchers, fresh veg," Carol began to heave. She then shrieked, "I AM NOT MADE OF STONE, I NEED LOVE AND AFFECTION." Carol released the crockery and grasped the sides of her head. In a whisper, she continued, "I want more; I need to have what I need for me." Carol was hitting herself in the chest, convincing herself of what she was saying while they looked on.

31.

Tracey jumped in a cab. She arrived late. "Ty, I am outside." Tyresse came outside, "Ready."

"Yep," she replied.

The choir sang the chorus in unified voices, "*Noel, Noel, Noel, Noel, born is the King of Israel.*" The sound drifted up to the ceiling and filled the spaces with melodious sounds. As the choir hushed to silence; the congregation's whispers grew and erupted into praise and worship unto the Lord. Tracey looked around her at individuals who appeared to be in a private audience with their maker.

Tracey shuffled into a pew. The church was full. The atmosphere was expectant, and ushers were busy filing latecomers into vacant seats. The church pastor's voice then bellowed out, "Blessed is our King Jesus Christ who was born to rid us of our sins." The whole congregation surged like a tidal wave at a football match, speaking in a language Tracey did not understand, and singing to God. She observed the excitement, the passion and adoration expressed by those present with her. One man got on his knees and smiled, waving his hands in the air. His lips were moving rapidly, and he appeared to be in a state of ecstasy. Tracey wondered if he was unaware of those around him or didn't care. People clapped and sang along with the singers who stood in front. Tracey enjoyed the music and danced along with the others. She felt drawn in by the jubilation. *Why were they so happy?*: she thought. They didn't appear to have a care in the world.

Tracey then spotted another blonde lady to the left in front and another with her hands raised in the air. No one seemed to notice she was white; they were too busy focused on singing and praying to God. Tracey did not really understand what was going on. She glanced at Tyresse and smiled. She observed that he was really getting into it. She held his hand and leaned into him. Tyresse motioned away slightly and sang to her. Tracey liked the attention and squeezed his hand. Tyresse gently released his grip and began clapping. Tracey felt as though she was left hanging like a spare accessory. She leant into him again. Tyresse jolted her to the side in an effort to express his dance unto the Lord.

"Did you enjoy that?" Tracey asked when they were leaving.

Tyresse looked at Tracey and knitted his brow, "This isn't a concert you know."

Tracey looked at him raising her eyebrow, "What?"

Tyresse strolled ahead of her, clapped his hands and swung to face her. "OK, what time are we all meeting up?"

"About one," Tracey replied.

"Tia and Archie are meeting us there," Tracey said.

"Xavier will be coming as well," Tyresse added.

Tia and Archie were already at the club. Tia was smoking outside when Tracey, Tyresse and Xavier strolled up to the entrance. Tia drew a long puff of her cigarette before throwing the stub on the ground. Tia greeted Tracey with a kiss and shook her head towards Tyresse and Xavier. They greeted her and strolled inside. Tracey looked across at Tia and walked in after them.

They all sat in a booth and Archie offered to get the first round. "So, what happened to you the other night?" Tia looking directly at Xavier.

Xavier glanced over at Tia, "I had to meet somebody."

"You didn't come back Xavier and left me in the flat with no light or heating." Protested Tia

Xavier looked surprised, "There wasn't?"

"Hell, no Xavier," Tia responded with a slightly raised voice. Xavier looked awkwardly at Tyresse, who was staring back at him.

Xavier then looked sternly at Tia, "What time did you get home then?"

Tia widened her eyes. "What time did I get home Xavier?" Xavier's expression was now fixed. He did not respond. "Xavier you left me there knowing you had no intention of coming back."

"That's not true," Xavier sighed, "Come on; drink up," grabbing Tia's drink off the tray and placing it in front of her. Xavier then stood up, grabbed his glass and wandered over to the dance floor. Tia sat with her mouth open and gazed at everyone around the table. Tyresse then invited Tracey to the dance floor. Archie sat quietly, wondering if he had missed the opportunity to jump to Tia's defence.

Tia began drinking. The more she swallowed, the more she forgot. She got up and strolled over to Xavier who was watching a young woman who looked across at him periodically. Tia began to dance in front of him. Xavier took a swig of alcohol, stepped forward and reached out for Tia. She welcomed his attention and pressed into him. Xavier led Tia through the club to the lavatories at the back. He pressed her to the wall.

"No way! what the heck are you doing?" Tracey yelled. Xavier took one step back; his flies were unbuttoned. However, all else was intact. Tracey led Tia outside.

"Tracey, what you doing?" Tia yelled. "You jealous because he wants me, the boy from the gentry's club," Tia laughed.

Tracey replied, "You what, Tia?"

"I just wanted to prove I could still have him," Tia continued, "He's nothing to me."

Tracey then said, "Why would you Tia, it doesn't make sense."

Tia laughed, "I know what I am doing, it's not just boys who have all the fun. I can do what I want when I like."

"Fun?" Tracey was angry. "You're drunk Tia, this don't make no sense."

Tia slowly turned around and said, "When your dad fucks you so hard you can't breathe while he's squeezing your neck and listening to you choke. When your daddy kisses you goodnight, while he is rubbing his penis against you, so Mummy doesn't see." She continued lamenting, "When Daddy threatens to press your naked butt up against the sweltering hot radiator if you tell."

Tracey took a short, sharp breath.

Tia then exhaled and lit a cigarette. "So, you see, I enticed Xavier. He came to me, to me Tray. I made him do my bidding."

"Tia, I am sorry, but it still doesn't make any sense."

"I survived Tracey. I hate who I am, he spoiled me, used me. I hurt so bad. Now men pay."

Tracey drifted over to Tia who was consumed in her own hell. "Tia let's go home."

"No!" Tia said indignantly, "I want to talk."

"OK, I am listening" Tracey had her hands up.

"I used to tell myself it was OK, just forget it happened" Tia paused, "Until the next time. Then it happened again and again and again and again and again, I never had a chance to forget about it." Tia spoke solemnly, "I used to feel guilty because I enjoyed it." I couldn't help it. I used to come over and over again. He enjoyed watching me come. I think it made him think I wanted it and invited him to violate me." She smirked. "What a pig." Tia looked at Tracey. Tracey sighed and broke eye contact briefly.

"When did it stop," Tracey asked.

"When a teacher asked me what I enjoyed doing the most, a year and a half after starting primary school," Tia then tightened her lips and dropped her eyelids. "He then went to prison, and I went into foster care." Tia then thought about Mum's stray boyfriend; the relationship was short-lived at the time; he acted swiftly, grooming her for his personal services.

"Why did you go into foster care?" Tracey asked.

"They didn't believe my mother never knew. I was so scared, sleeping in someone else's bed. I did wrong and was being punished again. It was a total nightmare. I used to smear the walls with shit. No one would come near me then. I thought they would send me home. Can you believe? How twisted was I?" Tia then took a deep breath. "I wonder how Aarti is doing in India. I hope she's OK,"

Tracey responded, "Yeah, I was thinking that yesterday."

"I was looking everywhere for you two; you OK?" Tyresse appeared concerned.

"We're fine," Tracey answered. Tia produced a fake smile and walked back into the club.

"Everything OK, Tray?" Tracey looked at Tyresse with a resigned look on her face and followed Tia.

32.

Xavier opened his eyes. It was Boxing Day. He looked around and rolled onto his back. He was sober and alert to the silence around him. He got up and opened the door to the fire escape. He peered out, observing passers-by in the street below.

He thought about his parents. His mother was disappointed that he had left just after Christmas. He had made an excuse and left. Xavier then lit a cigarette, smoked it and climbed back into bed. He checked his phone. Neither Tia nor Tyresse had called. He wasn't affected.

Xavier was of the opinion that the seasonal celebrations were based on a combination of Christian and pagan deities. Xavier sat speaking to himself, "Fools! They need to believe in something intangible to manage their suffering and to qualify their existence. The world's population is surplus to requirements; born needlessly into poverty, famine and disease." Xavier believed that the one world order agenda would remedy these maladies, creating utopia on earth.

Xavier studied his physique in the mirror. He pivoted on his toes, smiling at what he considered a muscular work of art. He imagined the fittest and strongest would be considered for the Cryogenic process in order to experience a rebirth into the new world structure, the future.

He imagined Tyresse as a superhuman, invincible and heroic. He smiled, speaking to himself, "Like me, a dynamic and resilient creature." His thoughts drifted to Tia. A wave of repugnance scented the air, he motioned his nostrils to the side; looking down he observed the broken pencil in his hand. He smiled. *Of no consequence:* he thought.

PING, a text arrived. It was Tyresse wishing him the best for the season and inviting him to church for the New Year celebration. exhaling slowly, he thought: *Ty, church? For you Ty, I just might...* Xavier chuckled to himself, breaking the pencil into smaller fragments.

Xavier sat thinking about his greatest conquests and how he was going to satisfy his craving for satisfaction; for dominance.

At times, he needed to feel emotion, however unsure of how or why? Ordinarily, he felt little compassion or empathy for others and questioned the motivation of their responses towards human tragedy or misfortune. He prided himself on his academic attainment and measured others against his own achievements. He observed Tyresse's attributes to be exotic, spontaneous and daring, abstract in comparison to his own.

"How do I get Aarti onside?" he whispered to himself, "How do I get her to love me, to want me? She is beautiful, desirable..." Xavier imagined her desiring him in secret. Waiting for the moment to confess undying love for him. Her integrity haunted him. He felt some emotion, some stimulation when thinking about her. "Is it love?" he asked himself. He admired her from a distance, afraid to discover her thoughts and feelings and to know his response. Xavier became anxious, uncertain. He sat so absorbed in his thoughts he missed Tia's call. His phone was on vibrate. He glanced at the phone and cast his vision upwards towards his right shoulder, plotting his next move.

Tia sighed, throwing her phone on the bed. *Maybe he's still asleep:* She thought: *It's early.* She had not slept, thinking about Xavier and how he would complement her life, coming from a rich family and a good home.

Tia shut her eyes blotting out thoughts of her conversation with Tracey last night. She felt sick to the stomach. She had drunk too much.

"Tia, coming down for some breakfast babe, Merry Christmas," her mother was smiling from the doorway of Tia's bedroom.

"Merry Christmas Mum," Tia smiled back. "What's for breakfast?"

"Full English," Faye replied.

"Coming." All Tia could think about was seeing Xavier.

33.

Tia and her mother sat at the kitchen table with mugs of tea. It was warm and cosy, the smell of left-over turkey dinner lingered in the atmosphere.

She observed the water boiling amidst fluffy cooked potatoes destined for the oven and a bottle of mulled wine and hot mince tarts on the sideboard.

"Who am I Mum?" she whispered.

"You're my little girl. What's brought this on?" replied Faye looking perplexed and slightly worried.

Tia leaned forward. "Why did you have me, Mum?"

"Because I knew you were going to be perfect." Faye smiled at Tia. Tia looked unconvinced. The scene around her represented Christmas at its best, perfect; however, she felt incomplete, tainted and alone in her suffering. She felt tormented by her feelings, unable to communicate the extent of her grief to others.

"Perfect! Mum, when you look at me what do you see?"

Faye then focused on the task at hand, "I see my baby all grown up. You're confident, strong and very loving." Faye then chuckled to herself, "You don't take any rubbish."

"What do you mean, don't take any rubbish?"

"People can't pull the wool over your eyes, you see right through them." Tia was not convinced of her mother's opinion, but accepted her mother's view, nonetheless, and laughed out loud.

Tia's stepfather walked into the kitchen and greeted them. Tia smiled back at him, thinking that he just represented another broken facet of her life. "You OK, Dad?" she asked, John, shook his head. "Good. She murmured under her breath. Tia resented John's silent confidence being a functional part of this family, seeing himself represented in each and every member but her. He was smug, assured of his authority in his own home. Tia felt sick, unable to establish her position as the oldest of three siblings.

"Dad, what happened to the angel on top of the tree?" Tia enquired.

"Oh, Abigail liked the golden star," he stressed, "It makes her happy."

"And the kitten?" John now hesitant, looked across at Faye, "Abigail and Aaron thought Cinders was a better name for her being grey and that." Tia stared at John. There was a pregnant silence. John then stood up and went back upstairs.

"How's Archie?" Faye asked.

"Fine, we've settled in," Tia replied. "Mum, why did you let them change Mr Muggles name?" John seemed invincible, no one could take her stepfather's power away. "You let them change his name."

Faye replied, "It's only a cat Tia, it's no big deal." Tia got up and went back to her room.

Staring out the window, Tia thought: *Why does no one take me seriously, or see me as a force to be reckoned with? Why do I always have to fight for respect?* Tears were now falling; Tia pressed her fingertips against the glass and leaned her forehead against the cold pane. She felt relief having to brace herself against the cold sensation sinking into her skull.

Tia was at a loss as to how she was going to overcome these battles.

Walking back into the kitchen she said, "Mum do you ever feel out of control, I mean not in control?"

"What do you mean T?" Faye looked puzzled shoving empty pans near to the sink.

"Do you ever wish you had a different life? Have you got what you wanted in life? Do you feel responsible for all the wrong in your life? And is it your fault?" Tia was now propelling forward, "What would you change and why?"

Faye looked over at Tia, "What's happened to you? What's all this?"

Tia stared at her mother. "Mum what do you think I am saying?"

Faye turned around. "I married because I loved your dad." Tia shot a glance at her mother. Faye recoiled, "I was a single mum. I had no education and no backing from my family, they were twisted, wrong. When I had you, a black baby, they disowned me. Well, I never felt wanted anyway, just another number that my mother could claim benefits for," she deduced, "I was only 15. Your dad accepted me and you, Tia. I struck it lucky with him. Can you imagine how hard it was for me then? I was on my own, an outcast amongst my own people." She continued, "Your dad was different. I thought about what it would be like to have my old life back. Anyway, We all know how that turned out."

Tia beckoned, "Are you saying that you regretted having me?"

"No Tia, never?" Tia could see the pain in her mum's eyes.

Truthingdom

"How do I really fit in this family Mum?"

Faye beckoned, "Your brother and sister love you, as I do."

"What about Dad?" Tia looked into her mother's eyes.

Faye drew breath, speaking in a low voice, "You know he loves you."

Looking into her mother's eyes Tia rebuked that statement, "No Mum he loves his own, that's the truth."

Faye sat back, "You're wrong." Faye now looked indifferent. Tia got up and went into her parent's bedroom. Her dad was watching TV. He peered down at her over his glasses.

Tia began, "I remembered something." John raised his eyebrows. "You never cuddled me or sat me on your lap."

John lay there watching Tia and said, "STOP, I know you think I don't love you and that I don't care about you, but it's not true. I have always loved you. After what happened..." He continued, "they'd accuse me next."

The room fell silent.

Tia responded, "You've always loved me; really?"

John got out of bed, "Look, Tia, don't come here spinning your axe looking for someone else to destroy. You have a short memory, my girl."

"What's going on here?" Faye startled John, who drew back and sat at the edge of the bed. Faye then added, "Is that how you felt John, it's her fault? Is that what you're saying?"

John sprang to his feet, "What do you mean by that?" Tia smiled as she brushed past her mother who was pressing her palms into John's chest. "Calm down John."

Tia promptly left the house and arrived, sometime later, at Xavier's house unannounced.

Xavier stroked Tia's arm as she lay asleep next to him. He looked at her beautiful face and thought, she's so messed up, I don't feel anything, nothing at all.

He lusted after her beautiful form. However, he despised her fragile emotions; weak. He rebuffed his own thoughts. He felt bare, not being able to fathom his own understanding of joy, peace, love... playing the part, however, was easy; praising his own efforts in arousing feminine wiles; evading detection.

He sat up. Tia roused. He looked down and smiled, "Morning." He then stood and marched over to the kitchen and switched on the kettle.

"What were you like as a little boy?" Tia enquired with a smile.

"Pleasant enough."

"Did you have any pets?"

"Mum had a dog,"

"What was its name?"

"Flint." He stood with an ambiguous smile on his face.

"What are your plans for the day?" Xavier asked.

"Nothing in particular," she said invitingly.

"I agreed to meet with friends in an hour," as he turned and headed towards the bathroom.

Tia was disappointed but knew it was pointless to press Xavier, she would only be disgruntled. "And later?" she shouted.

"Busy, sorry."

She was, nonetheless, accustomed to his offhand manner. She thought it to be 'his way', no biggie.

Shutting the bathroom door, Xavier thought: *Don't question me girl, get dressed.*

34.

A woman was screaming in the street, several men heckled after her. Aarti rushed to the window. The woman was on her knees crying, her hands cupped together, reaching out to the man in front of her. He continued to openly chastise her, hitting her about the head and chest. She cowered in an attempt to avoid the beating. He picked up a thin branch and began hitting her on her back. She cried out. The men gathered around were shouting, justifying the persecutor's actions. Aarti shouted out, "Stop, what are you doing?" Her father then appeared in the courtyard and ran out onto the street. He approached one of the men in the crowd. The man then ordered the persecutor to stop, and they all gathered together away from the victim, who knelt with her head bowed on the sandy road. The men spoke in muffled voices. Their animation spoke of conflict and hostility. Aarti's heart was beating rapidly. She wanted to run downstairs; however, she felt compelled to remain on the spot, her mind was racing ahead of her feet. She turned around and began running. She ran into her mother and drew back, apologising for the collision. Her mother gripped her arms and motioned her to a chair in the hallway.

"Let your father deal with this." Aarti's mother's eyes beckoned to her. Aarti could hear muffled screams and looked towards the doorway. Her mother tightened her grip, saying, "She defied her husband." Aarti's mother stepped back.

"Why? What did she do?"

"Her mother in law says she is willful and stubborn. She ran away from the house."

"But why?" Aarti enquired, "What did she do?"

Aarti's mother explained that the young woman had a baby recently and is struggling to cope with the expectations of motherhood and caring for her new husband and in-laws.

Aarti ran back upstairs and looked out of the window. The touts had resumed selling their products on the roadside. There were no signs of friction. Her father was talking to one of the men involved in the feuding earlier.

Aarti snatched her father away from the front door and sat him down alongside her on the sofa in the parlour.

"Bapuji, why was he beating her?"

Vishnu answered apologetically, "She is not meeting the expectations of the family. They paid a large dowry for her and expect that she will fulfil all their expectations of her."

Aarti was now appalled, "Bapuji, this is modern society, they cannot behave in this way."

Vishnu then said, "Beti, your mother knows what is expected of her. She is devoted to me and has given me you. I am grateful for our union and her companionship."

Aarti turned to her father, "So the dowry allows him to treat her like a chattel?"

Vishnu smiled at his daughter, "You young people, you are opportune with good fortune and favour. You are my pride and joy. The dowry ensures that her in-laws will provide for her. It is like a binding contract. All will be well, do not worry."

Aarti persisted, "Bapuji, what did you say to them?"

He told her, "I told them that this could be settled amicably. It was not appropriate to conduct themselves like this in the street." Her father then led her by the arm into the garden for lunch.

"Bapuji, do you believe that a girl's parents should still pay a dowry? Can you put a price on a woman's head?"

Smiling at her, her father said, "For you, I would pay a king's ransom."

"So, I would be captive?"

"No, protected," her father responded.

"What would I need to be protected from, Bapuji?"

"It seems the lure of the beast. Have you forgotten our traditions, our ways and adopted those you know little about?"

"Father total subjection is not living, allowing the puppeteer to spend your life force orchestrating his own will, his own desires."

"So, you question our values, discard what has served as an institution, guaranteeing a woman's right to birth nations, to exhibit pride in her creation and the fulfilment of having procreated to advance Krishna's sovereignty on the earth."

"I will need to purchase a car when I return, my explorations take me further and further afield, discovering my new habitat." Aarti's eyes rested on her mother's gaze.

"Habitat," her father scoffed, "That sounds like a jungle," her father appeared defiant.

"Which do you fear more Bapuji, me discovering the limitless powers of my own mind or you overcoming your own fears and limiting beliefs?"

"Beti, all life is reflecting back at you, tell me all that you can see," her mother waited expectantly. Aarti cast her eyes downward and paused for a moment.

"Maa, I am not judging, only considering the right of each individual to speak unto their own destiny, without interference, until one's true intention is known."

Her mother's voice now softened to a whisper, "I guided you away from the cliff's edge as a baby, I guided you away from the bad intent of others as a young girl, without interference you would have been lost to the jackal."

"Maa, the young are innocent and naive. It is the responsibility of the old to celebrate the nature, the very essence of the young and help them to discover themselves, their passions, what stimulates them." Aarti felt her heart palpitating. She desired to be free to be rid of her torment. Her head began to swirl, she was angry, her diaphragm expanded, her skin tingled, she could now feel the cool breeze and stood up. She exhaled as she walked out into the night air.

Aarti slipped out of the house in search of the woman she had pitied earlier. She recognised the woman, sitting outside on the porch; her contorted face frightened Aarti. Aarti stood in front of the woman's parents-in-law's home. She could not move forward, she stood there motionless, numbed with fear. "What am I afraid of?" her mother's words of wisdom came floating back to her. Was her fear this woman's jailer? Was she representative of the institution and playing out her part, muzzled and disarmed?

35.

"Tyresse," Brenda stood looking over at Tyresse, who was reading a newspaper at the kitchen table.

"Mum," he answered.

Brenda sat at the table. "When you were a teenager, I feared for your life; now that you are a man I pray for your future."

Formerly, Tyresse had spoken of his passions and had begun to manifest those ideas; however, each one was short lived. He had lacked the perseverance and stamina needed to pursue those goals and was becoming increasingly immune to fighting the odds to succeed and win.

Brenda's parents came to Britain in the sixties. They strived to elevate to the middle ground, owning their own business and acquiring property. They instilled in their daughters the mindset to maximise their own potential, to value the right to choose and liberty of mind in speech and expression.

Brenda had a strong sense of identity and self-worth and tirelessly strived to further develop an understanding of the value of these attributes by serving the needs of others through her career and personal deeds.

On reflection, she wondered if she had served her son less by pandering to his every whim; mollycoddling him until he approached manhood.

"Mum, I recognise my past failings, looking for a handout; thinking the world owed me something because my forefathers had been enslaved and downtrodden. Setting my generation back." He spoke up, "Mum when you're used to making quick, easy money a job seems..." He halted breathing out through his nostrils. He looked up, "It takes three weeks to change a habit of a lifetime. If you stay true to the process. Those minefields are hard, but low valleys can be scary, hopeless places where a man loses his soul. Mum, I want to live, to experience joy, not unhappiness."

Tyresse answered the phone. He heard Denzil running. He was panting frantically. "Where are you, man?" Tyresse drew away from the table, stood up and went upstairs to his bedroom.

Tyresse listened intently as his cousin spoke. "They onto me man. Shit, move, move, move," chatting away incessantly to himself. His breathing now was shallow and calculated.

Tyresse then said, "Where you now?"

Denzil responded, "In a hedge. They went to the flat looking for me. My Mum said they asked her to choose which weapon they should use and brought out lots of stuff. She was shaking. She just called me, told me to stay away. I was on the estate man, turning into my block. I turned and ran."

"Come here then, ennit" and hung up the phone.

"Where Denzil put the tings now?" Paulette searched in the hidden crevasses in his bedroom. "Me haf a pay de rent this month and buy me michinos for New Year's." She stood up cradling a handful of white rocks wrapped in plastic. "Make me call Tyresse."

Brenda had long since separated herself from Paulette, as their contrary views often clashed, sharing differing points of view regarding the means of survival and the differing sacrifices made to achieve this end.

Paulette's philosophy was that individuals had the right to choose how to live their life; answerable only to God. She saw authority as enforced control opposing freedom of expression. A person's karma; perhaps their destiny.

Brenda believed Paulette did not duly consider consequences severely enough to heed a downfall, yielding permanent repercussions. Nor thinking about the impact of drugs on a sociological level. Brenda wondered; where was her conscience, her desire to save or rescue humanity?

36.

Tracey strolled into the kitchen clutching a wet wash rag to her head. Carol was in the full throes of preparing Christmas dinner.

Dave sat at the table drinking coffee. "Morning sweetheart." Tracey did not reply, fetching a cup from the cupboard. Carol stole a glance before putting the stuffing in the oven. "You gone deaf or what?" he said.

Tracey finally responded. "Do you remember anything from last night?"

"Like what?" he responded.

"You slobbering all over Trina, making a fool of yourself."

"You what?" he responded looking perplexed.

"You embarrassed us all with your wayward behaviour," Tracey persisted, "Look at you; you were all over her like a punter on the kerb," Tracey now looking at her father with disgust. "Mum was humiliated, heartbroken; did you care?"

"Now wait a minute Tracey, how dare you speak to me like that." He turned snarling at Carol, "This is your fault, crying for sympathy like a yelping dog. You can't fight your own battles, so you turn my daughter against me."

Carol stood rigid, beckoning his mercy with bulging eyes. "I didn't say anything Dave."

Walking across the kitchen, Tracey said, "Don't apologise to him Mum, you did nothing wrong."

Whimpering, Carol said, "I didn't mean to upset anyone. Please stop."

"No Mum you did nothing wrong." Tracey lunged at her father, her fists clenched at her side.

Carol flung herself between them. "Stop making trouble Tray, go back to your black boyfriend and leave us alone." Carol clutched Dave's motionless arms behind her.

Neither Tracey nor her dad planned to strike out. Tracey just wanted to square up to him face to face. To let him know that she was not afraid. He would never have hit his little girl. His precious little angel.

Carol wanted Dave's approval. She convinced herself he needed her at that moment. Tracey was strong; everything she was not.

"What's his name Tray." Vince enquired from the kitchen doorway.

"Tyresse," Tracey replied, stepping away from her mother who then said,

"Are you pregnant?"

"No," Tracey declared ardently, "Why would you say that? Why mention it," glaring at her mother, "You knew what would happen." Tracey sighed, "I thought I was twisted, you're all afraid of what you don't know. Of what you don't understand. The joke is I'm on the outside too, I don't understand. I am trying to. It's all new to me too. I am standing between a rock and a hard place; an outcast here, a foreigner there."

Dave shouted, "Outcast, all of a sudden, since when Tray, now that you've gone with a coloured bloke?" Her father continued, "I didn't hear you rushing to defend Angie next door when she got into a fight with her brother at your cousin's party for bringing that Asian guy with her, or when your best friend thought she was pregnant by that gipsy boy. If I remember you kept schtum, never stood up for either of them; now all of a sudden because it's you, the rules are different. Yeah, think on that my girl."

Tracey attempted to fight back, "I never said anything, I didn't get involved."

Dave responded saying, "Yeah that's right, didn't defend either of them, you just stood there, right."

"Well, you did nothing to support any of them." Tracey snarled back at him.

"Now it's your turn you want us to jump for joy, you need to look closer to home mate." Dave, pointing his finger directly in her face.

Vincent stood up at the kitchen door looking emphatically at Tracey.

All was then silent. Tracey thought of her mother's ruthless outburst; perhaps a long-awaited vengeance of some kind. A woman possessed. Tracey looked up at her mother who was staring back at her. Tracey felt compelled to be quiet, watching for the next move. She then looked at her father who hung his head, as if trying to get around what had just happened. Vince then interjected, "What time is dinner Mum?"

"Around two babes," she replied walking away from the scene.

Tracey climbed slowly to the bathroom. This ritual was now becoming burdensome. Her throat ached. The pangs in her stomach persistently hurt. The magazines told her what to expect, she was on track. She told herself, just bear with it. The muscle spasms in her legs were painful as she tried to vomit bile. She was frustrated as very little surfaced in the toilet bowl. She stood on the scales which read 7st 8lbs. "I am getting close to my goal weight," she told herself.

"Tray, you in there?" her father softly knocking at the door.

"Yeah." Rising to her feet quickly, flushing before opening the door.

Dave asked, "Can we talk?"

"Yeah sure," she replied. They walked into the bedroom and closed the door. Tracey waited for him to start, not sure what to say herself.

"You know I love you Tray, you're my little girl." Tracey nodded. He continued, "I remember it like it was only yesterday. You sitting on my lap, playing games with your toys. I was so proud of you the first day at school, you didn't cry. You turned around waving your hands at me before disappearing inside the classroom." He then began looking around the room, rummaging for something to say. "I don't understand what happened," he said. "I gave you everything Tray. What more could I have done?" he began snivelling.

Tracey felt riddled with guilt and feelings of remorse as she watched him cry. She felt devastated. She was overcome with feelings of bewilderment. She felt 10 years old again, frantically looking for a way to abate his sorrows. Make him feel better. She then recalled singing, *down came the sunshine and brightened all the rain and …* as the song drifted from her mind, Mr Hyde appeared. Tracey jolted. Standing to her feet.

Dave was startled and looked directly up at her. She realised that she had been playing into his hands all this time. Manipulated! No one really cared about her happiness. Her stomach ached. She had been self- harming for years and never really understood why. She ran out the room, down the stairs into the front yard and briskly headed down the road.

Tracey's phone rang: "Tray, you there?"

"Yeah Tia, you alright?"

"Where are you Tray?"

"Still at home, but I am leaving in the morning. What a day I've had!" Tracey exclaimed,

"I've got a banging headache, dealing with my lot an all," Tia replied.

"Come over to mine for the rest of the holiday's Tray, we'll make good."

"OK, talk tomorrow."

37.

Xavier sat staring into the warm glow of his electric flame heater. He focused on the dance of the flames against the black parchment and observed the warm orange incandescence which covered the walls around him. He felt at peace with himself. He recalled his triumphs at boarding school; this aroused feelings of pride and gladness within him. He thought of Snubs, his best friend and how they would lob snowballs until their fingers were numb. He inhaled at the thought of roly-poly pudding and custard. He and Snubs always went up for seconds. Snubs would nestle up close to him at nights sometimes when he cried, to comfort him; at times arousing his nature when caressing him gently to sleep. Xavier remembered how gentle and caring he was. He felt intimacy reciprocated in those moments. He closed his eyes.

"What is love?" he said out loud. "Who is love?"

He thought: *I am powerful by default of my race, my upbringing, my gender. What should I fear?* For a moment he was convinced of his own greatness, all-powerful and lofty inheritance. He thought: *I am privileged amongst men. Why do I then doubt myself?* He reminisced: *I was always pristine, memorised my flash cards and sat still for Mummy. Her friends always patted me like a china doll. I stood to attention like a soldier when Daddy spoke, chewed quietly at dinner and slipped into bed with no fuss. A mundane, tidy life.* He smiled to himself thinking: *I aimed to please.* With little distraction, he sailed through primary school with flying colours. Mum and Dad were pleased.

Pulling the blanket around his shoulders, he thought: *Who do I please now?* recollecting the vastness of Huntingdon School for Boy's main hall, embellished with a coat of arms, parquet flooring and sparse oak wood furnishings which were complemented by ruby-coloured drapes, hanging alongside broad Georgian windows.

The pupils gathered together in the great hall; a sea of burgundy blazers sat in symmetry for assembly. He assimilated with them while chanting the declaration: "Treat others as you want to be treated."

He was taught to strive for excellence. To expect the greatest, to be the very best. He valued these mantras. It gave him direction, purpose. Praise was limited, and pleasing others guaranteed nothing, perhaps warranted a favour.

Out loud he uttered, "I love you unconditionally, I love only you." Staring into the firelight, his eyes danced in synchronicity with the flickers of the flames.

Xavier looked at the photographs scattered on the floor beneath him. He focused on a photo of him and Snubs fishing at summer camp. He laughed, thinking they had so much fun. There was another group photo of the boys of Tempest house, some of whom he still maintained contact with.

Snubs joined the Air Force and has been on active duty for the past four years. Xavier missed him. Taking a deep breath, he leaned back against the sofa.

Xavier heard a knock at the door.

"Hey, come in," He greeted Tyresse with a hug and a handshake.

"What you up to?"

"Chilling with a glass of wine, do you want some?"

"Sure," Tyresse looked down at the photographs. "Reminiscing about the old days?"

"Yeah, something like that, anyway what brings you round?"

"Got a spot of trouble with Denzil; owed dough, beaten up, badly."

"What!" Xavier threw himself back in the chair.

"Police were asking questions, am going to see him today, find out what the story is, man."

"Yeah, yeah."

"Anyway, what you been doing?"

"Just thinking."

"Yeah about what?"

"Life is complicated Ty, loving someone," Xavier was shaking his head.

"Yea, I know about that one."

"How's Tracey?"

"Yeah, she's good man."

"You still messing with Tia?"

"Tia's messing with me."

They chuckle amongst themselves.

"Seriously, you're not into her then?"

"Tia doesn't know what she wants, we're both lost souls in the universe."

Truthingdom

"This is going to end messy."

"You're reading too much into this Ty."

"So, you're just emptying your bags?"

"We've got an understanding."

"According to Tray, Tia says you two got this on lock."

"We're on different wavelengths, mate."

"Oohh, no, this is all twisted up," Tyresse continued, "She really likes you, man."

"Can't deal with all that." shaking his head.

"So, what you going to do?"

"Tell her she's got it confused. She's a whore."

Tyresse chuckles, "Nah man."

Xavier pandered to the audience, "A tramp, nothing special."

Later that night Xavier flexed his muscles in the mirror, admiring his frame. He then whispered to himself, "I'll make her beg me to stay."

38.

Tia gripped tightly to her emotions. She wasn't going to break down. Who would help her pick up the pieces?
She left her mother and step-father in their bedroom and hurried to her own room.

In her own space, alone, she dared to reminisce about her abuser, her mother's ex-partner. She thought: *Why did he do this to me? He said I was his special little girl. Did that make it right? No! No!*

She was now angry, thinking: *Why for so long? I remember sitting on his knee, I was five, six. At thirteen I hated myself for being stimulated, allowing him to continue, keeping it our little secret. Why?*

Tia could not make sense of what she saw as her decision to prolong what was unnatural: which part, the physical pleasure, the incest or the secret?

Can I be normal? How do I love now? Why do I love? Do I love or is it pretence? Why do men treat me the way they do? Could it be me? What do they see when they look at me?

What do I let them see when they look at me? This particular question resonated with her. Am I putting on a show, letting them see that I am in control and cannot be affected by them and their antics, their games? Or is that the way I choose to see it, to protect myself? She looks up in frustration. Angrily, she says to herself, "I allow Xavier to treat me the way that he does." She lowers her voice to a whisper, "No, I am in control, I allow him to affect me this way." She darts her eyes around the room, "How do I heal?" Floods of tears follow.

Later that afternoon, Tia joins her mum in the living room. "Mum", she says, "I want to get help."

"What do you mean?" She draws closer to Tia.

"Professional counselling Mum," she continues "I am going mad trying to figure out who I am."

"OK, Tia, I'll make an appointment in the morning." Faye was relieved, she didn't know how to help Tia.

Faye had struggled not knowing or understanding anything about black cultural heritage. She met a black guy at her local pub and had a brief affair. She knew a couple of black girls at school, but they weren't lifelong friends or anything. She gave birth to a beautiful baby girl and raised her in isolation for the most part, within the confines of her own limited understanding of her daughter's racial heritage and social exclusion.

She met a bigot who showered her with attention, who preyed on her low self- esteem and loneliness. She was grateful for his affection and the attention given to her only beloved mixed-race child.

As time passed, her prison without walls was erected, and Tia fell victim to abuse. He orchestrated Faye's daily regime with militant precision. She craved his affections and pandered to his sexual depravities. Tia had been groomed from very young and kept his secrets. Her mother claimed she never knew about the abuse and left him the moment social services became involved. Faye struggled with the fact that her child had been abused, questioning Tia as to when and where these encounters had taken place. Faye then felt guilty when Tia cross-examined her about whether she believed that Tia had been abused. Faye was devastated, not being able to protect her innocent baby girl. She had failed. Faye then persisted in fighting on *'Team Tia'* when needs be; while Tia forged a family of her own on the streets.

39.

Denzil arrives at Tyresse's home. Tyresse's mum is unaware of the situation and welcomes Denzil with a kiss.

Tyresse ushers Denzil upstairs to his room. The phone rings, "Ty, its aunty Paulette. Denzil wid you?"

"Yes aunty," Tyresse was well aware of his mother's views about Aunty Paulette and sighed.

"He lef de food ere you know, him not going to get dem money without selling de tings,"

"OK, aunty." Tyresse feels compromised. "Denzel, what you gonna do?"

"Tyresse shift the *rocks* for me until I'm in the clear. Things are hot right now Ty." Tyresse is shaking his head and tells Denzil he isn't game. Denzil is angry, "They're gonna kill me, man. You're my blood. I thought you had me, man." He walks out.

Tyresse is worried. Brenda asks if everything is OK, as she heard raised voices. Denzil slammed the door on the way out.

Denzil arrives back home. "What you doing 'ere Denzil?" his mother protests.

"I ain't got no choice. I have to sell the food to pay T dot back." In the meantime, youngers who had been watching the flat, fed back to the olders that he had returned home.

They knock, Denzil stumbles back. They bundle him out. His mum is shouting, "Leave him." Denzil's younger siblings, 5 and 7 years old, watch seemingly unaffected by the commotion.

Denzil observed a machete and a five-inch blade flash as he is marched down the stairwell. The imprisoners took him to a house and began to torture him. "Where's the money?" They tied him to a chair. They punched him all over with knuckledusters and kicked his shins. Blood was now mixed with sweat. There were open cuts above his left eye, his back and chest. He told them that Tyresse had the food. "Call him," one of the men hand him his phone. His hands were bludgeoned and lacerated with defence wounds. His hands trembled as he made the call.

"Ty, bring the food, or they're going to kill me," Denzel was crying, Tyresse could hear the fear in his voice, he was pleading for Ty to bring the food now.

Tyresse took a cab and left without hesitation. When he arrived at the destination, he got into another car at the agreed meeting place. As he climbed in, he noted that all the boys wore balaclavas. The vehicle then sped into the night. One man sitting in the back shoved a black bag over his head and told him it was for his own safety.

When they got to the house, Tyresse was bundled through the door.

Denzil was being held at gunpoint. The curtains were purposely drawn not to give away the location.

Tyresse handed over the drugs and asked to leave with Denzil.

"No, he owes dough."

"How much?"

"£5,000"
Tyresse threw his eyes up. Denzil shot a stare at Tyresse then threw his body forward from the waist down, between his legs, as his hands were tied behind his back. Tyresse could see that his back was severely bruised.
Swollen dark patches exhibiting darker crimson purple.

All the imprisoners wore balaclavas, and he did not recognise any of their voices.

"Give me a couple of days, I'll have the money," Tyresse said, head up straight, chin slightly raised, staring the ringleader in the eyes.

"You have till Thursday at 4 o'clock."

Tyresse's contacts were futile. In desperation, he contacted Xavier who was unable to loan him the money. He sold coke to Xavier once a month, Xavier used a sizeable amount of his monthly allowance to feed his habit.

Tyresse turned to his mother as a last resort. Brenda lamented, she struggled to submit, as she could ill-afford this debt, and Denzil's mother stated that she had no money.

Brenda was resentful of her half-brother's child for creating a risky situation which endangered the family, especially during these austere times, when parents and even nurses are using food banks.

Brenda gave Tyresse £3,000. She needed to borrow some of the money herself to raise what she did.

Tyresse was able to raise the remainder of the money, in bits and drabs on top of what his mother gave him.

The capturers arranged a meeting place in a remote industrial park; counted the cash and left Denzil for dead in a dumpster.

"He's in there," one of the hooded men pointed.

Tyresse alerted the police and ambulance services, who arrived within 15 minutes. It seemed like a lifetime. Denzil appeared unconscious. Tyresse screamed out his name then his eyes rolled back. He was badly beaten up. Tyresse called out to God, "Please Lord save him. Please!"

Tyresse's heart was racing, and he was shallow breathing very quickly.

They arrived at A&E shortly before Denzil's mum. Brenda had arrived 30 minutes after the ambulance.
Several of Denzil and Tyresse's friends had arrived and gathered in the foyer. The police had come and began questioning Tyresse in the waiting area.

Denzil flatlined. His mother screamed, "My baby, Oh God, no." She threw herself over him. Nurses jostled to lift her away. Tyresse dived from beyond the curtain and effortlessly cradled her and elevated her body.
The doctor was rubbing the pads, whilst a nurse ripped open Denzil's shirt. Tyresse and Denzil's mother stumbled backwards in the commotion. The pads made contact with his chest, and his

chest rose and fell back. The doctor did this several times. Nothing. Denzil's mother screamed.

Tyresse let her go, and they fell to the floor. 'Beep …. Beep, beep. All eyes settled on the resuscitator. They had faint a pulse; Denzil had died for several minutes.

Denzil's mother was breathing erratically, her chest heaving up and down, her hands quivering by her side. Her face was wet and her hair dishevelled. "Thank you, Lord, thank you for sparing my baby's life. Don't let him go, Lord, hold on to him Lord. You are the great healer, the physician, the miracle worker. You are the Alpha and the Omega, the great High Priest." She gasped for air and continued giving thanks and praise.

The registrar squeezed passed, ordering the nurses to remove everyone from the cubicle space.

Once clear of the cubicle, Brenda leaned into Tyresse, squeezed his arm and cried silently. Tyresse stood still with his head bowed while their friends murmured amongst themselves close by.

The police swiftly approached Tyresse again and asked for his account of the situation. Tyresse informed the police that Denzel had called him and told him that he was in trouble and his location. The police pressed for more information. However, Tyresse was unable to assist. A 'snitch', an informer, talking to the feds, would only be wishing ill upon themselves and worse damnation for their children, close family and friends.

40.

Tracey tossed and turned throughout the night, thinking about how she was going to deal with her parents. Her mum was clearly not an ally and Dad just ignored her, "How dare they judge me," she said out loud. "He's a lovely guy; funny, smart, looks pukka. They don't even know him."

Tracey avoided thinking about what her father had said about not readily denouncing racism before she met Tyresse. She focused for a minute. It was true, she acknowledged, that she had never addressed the issue head-on, never had to deal with it or been confronted with it. She had no choice now and felt harassed by the idea of having to deal with it. "Tyresse is worth it." She then realised that she was falling in love.

"Upminster to Ealing Broadway" the tannoy speaker rang out above Tracey's head on the platform. She was heading to Pimlico to stay over at Tia's for the remainder of the holidays.

Archie greeted Tracey with open arms. She took a deep breath and invited the delicious smells to massage her nostrils. She smiled and fell into the arms of Tia who was clutching a glass of white and thrusting another glass towards her.

"Thank you." Tracey was grateful to be there. As she looked around the cosy warm living room, she observed soft vintage lighting, soft jazz music playing in the background and snow on the rooftops beyond the window pane. She slumped into a nearby chair and sipped on her wine.

"Tracey, wake up." She smiled. Tyresse and Xavier were standing above her. They began singing out loud, and she laughed, smiling in her heart and felt at home with them all for the first time in her adult life away from home. She sighed and whispered to herself, "I miss you, Dad."

They all enjoyed dinner; Archie was an excellent cook and took delight in the compliments received. While washing up, Tia looked over at Tracey, "Tray can I ask you something?"

"Sure."

"I've started seeing a counsellor about all my shit." She let out a huge sigh, her chest hurt. "I mean I want to feel good about myself, I wanna love who I am, I wanna be significant, important, meaningful to me, to others." She continued, "I just don't want to be seen as a fake, pretending to be brave, hard, fearless. Inside I am scared shitless of finding out who I really am." Tia turned away.

Tracey looked behind her to check if the others were looking and slowly walked up to Tia and gripped her shoulder. She leaned into Tia and whispered, "Make room for me on that couch."

Tia looked over her left shoulder and smiled at Tracey, who was laughing heartily at her. They both laughed and began flicking water at one another.

Tracey stayed over at Tyresse's house that night. Brenda greeted Tracey with a hug and wished her the best of the holiday season.

While relaxing in the bedroom, Tyresse focused his attentions on Tracey. "Tray, can we talk," Smiling back at Tyresse, she listened in anticipation. "Don't be angry, OK?"

"Why?"

"I heard you last night."

"What?"

"Vomiting again in the bathroom, what's going on? You not eating again or what?"

Tracey looked bewildered, she was afraid, she thought: *what should I say?* "I'm not sure, I might be pregnant,"

"What!" Tyresse was on his feet. "You what?" his face now contorted. She looked up at him. She began hyperventilating while making efforts to take deep breaths.

"I am not sure Ty, I gotta take the test."

Tyresse was frowning with his palms facing upwards. He sat down and stared in front of him. "Right, you need to take the test tomorrow, OK?"

"Yeah, OK." Tracey was now in panic mode. She was finally confronted with her nemesis incarnate right before her eyes. She thought frantically: *What do I do, what can I say? I can't tell him the truth.* She was ashamed, until now this was her power, although it was painful, it helped ease the pain, made her feel dominant over circumstances that she could not control.

She felt compromised, exposed.

"Tray, it will be OK," Tyresse's face now relaxed. "We will deal with the situation."
Tracey looking around the room, she focused her gaze on Tyresse. *No*: she thought: *I can't tell him. He would be disgusted with me. Maybe he would think I am twisted in the head. Drawing that kind of attention to myself would be selfish.*

Tracey fell asleep. She was tired as she had not slept or eaten very much the previous evening. Tyresse, staring at the TV, drifted into thoughts about Denzil's close call with death.

Brenda popped her head around the bedroom door calling out to Tyresse, "Are you listening to me Tyresse?" He snapped out of his thoughts and turned to face Brenda. "The police are here,"

"Why?"

"They want to talk to you."

"What about?"

"I don't know."

The police were stood in the doorway. "Good evening" Tyresse nodded. "We wanted to know if you had any more information about the assault. Remembered anything else?"

"No." Tyresse was consumed with apprehension. The police officers looked on intently.

One of the officers then said. "Denzil told us you were the first to arrive on the scene and found him."

"Yeah" slightly shaking his head.

"Did you see anyone else?"

"Why all these questions?" Brenda stood behind Tyresse with an uneasy demeanour, recalling past encounters with an officer named Dobs, she knew him well. He was the local bobby, usually cordial; however, an unwelcome visitor.

Tyresse's inherent dislike for the police stemmed from past encounters on the streets of Enfield, where *stop and search* was commonplace. The power dynamics rendered him impotent to defend, to resist. This suppressed his wilful soul force. Non-visible chains.

He understood their mandate to defend and protect, to stop crime; however, he questioned their deep-seated nature, fashioned and influenced by their own life experiences, their own prejudices. Could the two be inexplicitly divided, separated; namely their duty and their innate responses? Which nature is in operation, what can be trusted, when confrontation is in the mix; that could be said of both parties? In his mind, the police rule over all; regardless.

The officer then responded, "We're asking all these questions in order to understand what has happened." Tyresse's body language exhibited an air of wariness.

They left.

Brenda questioned the further intrusion, keen to know the unsaid. Tyresse was, however, dismissive of her enquiries.

41.

"Will you marry me, be my wife?"

Aarti froze, then responded saying, "We do need to talk." She needed time to process this.

Ajay looked disappointed, "Our families have been arranging this for months."

"I know," mindful not to say anything else for fear of disapproval. Aarti noted Ajay's mother stared intently from a distance whilst chatting to Aarti's mother in the garden.

"Don't you want me?"

"Ajay, I have my studies in London for a year. In that time, we can become better acquainted."

"Are you saying no?"

"That is not what I am saying."

"I want for us to be married and for me to join you in Britain. You delaying will be frowned upon Aarti. We can be happy together Aarti."

Aarti took a deep breath in. "Just give us time Ajay."

Prema strolled through the doorway with her intended, they were a little early for dinner. Her parents followed close behind. Veer walked over, greeted Ajay and snatched a lingering gaze at Aarti. He sat next to Ajay, smiling intently at Aarti. Veer asked, "Ajay, where have your travels taken you this year?"

"To the south on business," Ajay replied.

Veer interjected, "Oh, I meant on vacation."

Ajay hesitated, "No in India."

Veer, looked at his shoes, vaguely interested, "Oh I see." Veer diverted his attentions to Aarti, "I was just admiring your necklace Aarti," examining every inch of her neckline. "You have good taste." Aarti thanked him for the compliment.

Ajay sat flustered wanting Aarti to himself. "Aarti, would you like another drink?"

"No thank you, Ajay," raising her full glass.

She then enquired, "Where did Prema get to?" casting her eyes around the garden. However, Prema was nowhere to be seen.

Aarti turned her body looking around her, hoping to be rescued. Alas, no one came. She turned, "Ajay, do you have any hobbies?" clutching at something to talk about.

"Yes, I enjoy playing cricket in my free time."

"Ahh right," she replied. The atmosphere felt like lead.

"What's yours?" Veer asked.

Aarti was caught unawares. "I am looking for new adventures, new experiences." She was pleased with her response.

"New stimulus then," Veer was smiling. She stretched a smile and looked across to Ajay who was watching Veer.

Prema then appeared, stating, "I didn't see your cigars in the car, are you sure you brought them out with you, Veer?"

"I am sure," he replied. "Never mind, I'll have to do without them."
Veer smiled at Aarti. She was irritated, thinking he lied.

Aarti lay in bed that night wondering how this was all going to turn
out. She was a far cry from making any decisions relating to
marriage and convinced Veer was a mistake waiting to happen.
She shuddered when considering how calculated he was and
whether he loved anyone but himself.

Ajay and his family were coming for lunch the following day. Aarti
was anxious thinking about what to say. What were their
expectations and how soon?

During the night, Aarti became restless. She was running through
the forest late at night. Her attacker was catching up. She was
afraid. He was on her heels. She screamed out and sat up in bed.
No one heard her. She was perspiring and felt clammy. She lay
back wishing this persistent nightmare would stop.

The next day, Aarti greeted her future mother in law, Yukti, "Good
afternoon. How are you this afternoon?"

"Fine," she responded in a calm and quiet voice. Ajay promptly
greeted Aarti and joined his mother on the sofa. Aarti served Chai
with Gulab Jamun. Aarti's mother knew Ajay's father enjoyed this
delicacy. Yukti led the conversation, "Ajay tells me about his
discussions with Aarti last night, about the marriage." She directed
her conversation at Aarti's mother. Aarti looked round at her
mother.

"Yes, it has been a topic of conversation," Aditi's response, cool
and reserved.

Vishnu interjected, "So what next?" Aarti felt faint. Ajay moved to
the edge of his seat whilst Ajay's father continued to gorge on the
sweet appetisers before him.

Yukti then persisted, "Shall we set a date?" At that moment Ajay's father began choking, coughing and spluttering everywhere. Yukti jumped up and ran across to assist Aditi, who was already beating on his back. Aarti slipped out of the room, catching her every breath. She ran into the garden and dropped to her knees.

"Sakhya Bhakti," she whispered, "help me, please help me." She began to cry. She moved deeper into the garden to avoid being seen. Aarti could then hear her mother calling her. Her mother sounded upset, she was running. Aarti stepped out of the shade.

"Mother, I am here?" We have called Dr Acharya to tend to Ajay's father. He responded to the smelling salts. He is breathless.
Aarti raised her hands and gazed up to the heavens, then ran in behind her mother.

Later that evening Aarti sat with her father in the garden. It was cool and quiet. The stars shone close by in the indigo sky, and Vishnu lay resting in the hammock.

Vishnu was shaking his head, "Thankfully, we have a doctor who is a neighbour." He continued, "He is recovering at home, give all thanks to Lord Dhanwantri." Aarti nodded her head in agreement.

Aarti sat still, examining her own feelings. Her instincts confronted her; apprehension, unease. She was afraid, nonetheless, wanting to speak out.

"Father, did you love Mum before you married her?"

"Why are you asking that my daughter? Your mother was beautiful, many suitors wanted to marry her," he laughed and settled again.

Aarti fidgeted, "Father did she love you?"

Her father turned to face her, his expression, searching, "It is OK to be nervous, it's a new chapter in your life. Your mother and I have secured land for you both nearby here, as a wedding present. I wasn't going to tell you, keep quiet, your mother will kill me." Aarti was now looking at him, her brows slightly knitted. He smiled back and lay down, nestling himself into position. Aarti was looking at him disheartened. She thought him oblivious to her anxieties.
Her mother was on the phone talking incessantly to Yukti.

"Prema,"

"Aarti," She was relieved Prema answered the phone.

"You OK? what a commotion this afternoon, your poor mother looked as if she was going to have a heart attack and began examining the food."

"Yeah,"

"Aarti, you OK, what's up?"

"I am thinking about this marriage thing."

"What do you mean?" Aarti took a deep breath. "He is handsome, eligible, quite a catch. His father's company won the award for up and coming new business this year. Count yourself lucky. Are you nervous Aarti? It's OK. I for one am not nervous, this is a good match; I am pleased with my parents' choice." Aarti was tongue-tied. "You there, Aarti?"

"Yes, I was listening to you."

"So, don't worry, all will be well."

The Conception

Aarti felt like a prisoner of her own circumstances or those put upon her. She knelt and prayed for deliverance.

"A date has been set for the wedding," Aarti's mother rushed into the bedroom. "In the summer, when you return, I am so excited," she tumbled at Aarti's feet. She continued, "There is so much to do, where do I start? What would I wear?"

Aarti sat staring at her mother. She was unable to speak, she just sat there. *What do I want? :* she thought: *Am I OK with this?*

She was due to return to Britain in three days. She felt nauseous, trapped. Ajay was a respectable man and deserved the very best. She thought: *What am I thinking? Do I want this? My heart says no, my head says wait. I need to think this through. He offers me security, love, affection, kindness and a family. Am I showing ingratitude? Many would take my place. Then why am I sat here trying to convince myself that this is what I want, what I need? Shouldn't I know what I want?*

She was unresolved. Unable to persuade herself of what she thought was the right thing to do. She perceived herself to be selfish, thinking only of herself when there was so much more to consider: *Can I think about my own happiness? Is that fair?*

42.

"How was India?" Xavier was stumbling over his words, clearing his throat, he felt challenged to continue, "Did you have a good time?" He shuffled in his seat. He was slightly annoyed; overwhelmed with feelings of shyness. He sat up, straightening his neck, engaging eye contact.

"It was great! I relaxed and ate loads," she lied but felt that a loaded response would suffice. "What did you do during the hols Xavier?" diverting attention from herself.

"Spent time with family and met up with the other guys last weekend."

His lingering gaze made Aarti blush; she got up and browsed around the fruit basket. She joined the queue; while caressing her midriff, she closed her eyes and took a deep breath. She began blowing out, and her hands started shaking. She placed the apple on the counter and walked quickly out of the canteen and out of the building.

"Aarti you OK?" she swung around. Tia walked quickly towards her and put her arms around her.

"I couldn't breathe, I felt faint," Tia stood with her until she composed herself. Tia steered Aarti into the canteen. She spotted Xavier, who looked a little confounded as they approached.

"Everything OK, Aarti?"

"Yes, perfectly fine, just felt faint that's all." She appeared flushed.

Why now, Aarti thought, with Xavier watching. She sat quietly hoping not to be noticed. Xavier placed a cup of tea in front of Aarti. She looked up and heard herself say. "Thank you." Xavier sat in front of her and smiled gently. Tia focused her attention on Aarti, thinking about her secret and whether that had caused her upset this morning.

"Would you like something to eat?" Xavier said in a gentle voice.

"No, thank you," she said hurriedly, hoping he would stop and leave her alone. Not that she didn't want the attention. She just felt weak and vulnerable right now. Tyresse walked in with Tracey and sat at the table.

Tyresse then asked, "Everyone OK?"

Xavier responded saying, "Yeah fine." Both Aarti and Tia looked up nodding their heads in agreement. Tracey stared at Aarti, noting her distorted grin through her teeth, and said nothing.

Tracey then said, "We all getting the train, yeah?"

All responded saying "Yes."

Archie prepared a vegetable meal for dinner. He loved to cook. He worked as a pastry chef in central London where they prepared and served à la carte meals. He would often bring leftover meals home. Tia enjoyed the desserts too. Xavier brought Aarti a glass of wine, she put her hand up, "Sorry, but no thanks."

"A glass of water instead?"

"Yes, thank you."

"So, what did you enjoy most about India?"

"India is my home; I love everything about it."

"Oh yes, of course," feeling stupid he attempted to recover quickly. "Was it very hot?"

"Yes," throwing her eyes up, thinking: *couldn't he think of something more original to say?*

"Do you have any hobbies, Aarti?" Xavier was now more relaxed.

"Yes, supporting women's charities back home; you know, servicing the needs of those without a voice, those who are oppressed."

"Right." Shaking his head; an almost absent response. He thought it sounded clichéd.

"It's gratifying, liberating," Aarti added, observing the vacant response. She felt the need to convince him of her passion and the worthwhile cause. "Do you not see the importance of freeing another from torment?"

He responded quickly, "Yes indeed," as if woken out of a stupor. Aarti was not convinced; this agitated her.

He then insisted, "Tell me more." She suddenly felt guilty, she thought perhaps she had misjudged him and proceeded to tell him about some of her encounters, including the incident in the street outside her family home. Tia then appeared and sat quietly alongside Xavier. He was listening to Aarti intently now and didn't notice her sitting there. Tia, content to listen, did not distract the conversation.

Across the room, Tyresse turned to Tracey on the sofa, "That was a close call."

"Yeah, what I relief, I am not pregnant," Tracey then asked, "How come you've never asked to meet my folks?"

"Have you told them I am black?"

"Yeah,"

"OK."

Tracey then looked intently at Tyresse, not knowing what to say next.
She then said, "Alright, what about next weekend?"

Tyresse smirked, "You're not ready for that Tracey."

"Why do you say that?"

"Was everybody pleased when you told them?"

Tracey was hesitant, "No, but, they know?"

Tyresse took a deep breath, "Can you handle them rejecting me on the spot, to my face with you standing there, Tray? What if one of us flips out? What would you do?" He persisted with this line of enquiry, "What if they rejected me?"

Tracey did not have a ready answer to any of the questions posed. She then thought: *We have only been dating for 6 months. How well do I know him? Is this going to last? Do I want to embrace his culture; be the only white girl in the ring? Did that matter really? What am I trying to convince myself of?* She threw her head back, as if shaking the weight of these thoughts off.

Tia, bored with what she considered small talk, interjected saying, "You glad to be back Aarti?"

"Ah, yes," Aarti replied.

Xavier looked wide-eyed at Tia, as if annoyed by the intrusion, and said, "Having lived in Britain for only a few months," darting a stare back at Aarti, "What experiences have impressed you the most?"

Aarti sniffed perspiration in the air. It was warm, "Well, clothes shopping." She struggled, "The architecture, excuse me." Aarti got up and went to the bathroom.

In the bathroom, Aarti took slow deep breaths. She had begun to suffer anxiety attacks since the rape and took time to calm herself in the bathroom. She had hot flushes and removed her sweater. Her thin blouse allowed air to pass through. She was grateful.

Tia leaned forward, "Would you like another drink, Xavier?"

"Yes, thanks."

Tia handed Xavier another glass, "What you been up to? Haven't heard from you this week."

"I've been busy Tia."

Tia looked closely at Xavier, observing his dismissive attitude. She smiled to herself, thinking, "Is this what you deserve, wow, he really thinks he is all that. I so have my own drama going on, I don't need this." She switched the conversation, "Finished all your assignments?"

He sighed and looked across at her, "I have one or two to finish."

Tia nodded her head in acknowledgement. "Hopefully, you'll meet the deadlines." Tia then slowly stood up and walked across to Archie.
Xavier studied her curvaceous figure as she walked away.

Aarti returned, "Sorry, had to go,"

"That's OK," Xavier adjusted the cushions where she was seated.

"So, what about you?" Aarti asked,

"What about me? There's not much to tell."

"Your family, where you come from?" Aarti persisted.

"I am an only child, I went to boarding school, travelled a bit and still trying to make sense of my life."

"Which part?" Aarti smiled at him. "You make it sound so uninteresting."

"Which part was interesting or made sense?"

"You decide."

"Oh, right, ah, I liked riding horses and winning polo matches,"

"Which part are you trying to make sense of?"

"My feelings,"

"Are you happy?"

Xavier paused, realising how quickly Aarti had targeted his inner sanctum. "Sometimes."

Both then sat quietly with a prolonged silence. Aarti then whispered, "You are easy to talk to; allow yourself to just live in the moment, embrace and feel how you are feeling,"

Xavier sat still, staring at one spot on the floor. He laughed, "Are you a guru?"

"No way, in India there are many wise men; just listen to what your heart is telling you, don't be afraid,"

Xavier wanted to fall into her arms. He felt safe and content following the smooth monotone in her voice.

43.

Tia visited Constance. It had been some time since they had last seen one another. Constance recently had had a baby girl and was planning to marry her childhood sweetheart.

"What's up T?"

"I'm scared to trace my dad; he might not want to know me."

"You scared he might reject you? Tia, you have to look past the fear and face him head-on."

"You're brave, man, I'm not sure I can."

"Right now, you don't even really know what you're afraid of, do you?"

"I might not even like him, I might regret even trying,"

"Right now, you're guessing, you don't even know how you would react. You can't deny yourself the right to know for yourself."

"I'm even struggling with knowing who I am, Am I black? Society tells me I am, but I'm white too, right?" Tia shakes her head unconvinced of anything for sure.

"Tia look at me!", Constance instructed, "You need to break this down. I've known you since we were young, and I know what I'm looking at,"

"What's that?"

"A strong, beautiful queen, who doesn't stand for no nonsense. My sister. Tia you can't allow society to dictate to you who you are. You need to feel what you're comfortable with. Who you are deep down. Where is your joy, Tia? Validate yourself. Tell others who you are and love those loving you. Come on, give me some love," The two embraced and cried together. "Would you be my daughter's godmother?"

"What! Yeah, of course."

Tia always knew Constance to be established and steadfast in her racial identity and cultural expression, although mixed with British urban culture. Tia was slightly envious of Constance, her racial identity, her heritage; being validated over and over by her extended family.

On the way home, she thought about the people in her life, her interpersonal relationships and how meaningful they were. She thought about those she loved and those who loved her and the alienation from her mother's family. She didn't feel any pain about being rejected by them as she never knew any different. She just noted the unfairness of the situation, being shunned for being different.

She thought: *Should I then despise them for judging me so unfairly? Should I then excuse their ignorance, their prejudice? Should I reach out to them? If they meet me, they might accept me and show me the love I have been denied all these years. Do I need them to validate me though?* Tia grappled with these questions for days not knowing what she should do. She hoped that she would be able to focus her attention on her inner feelings without fear of being lost or overwhelmed during her first counselling session. She had, in fact, had this epiphany before, needing and wanting to explore her inner feelings. Her sisters in the hood confided in family and friends, as did their parents, not forgetting the local pastor; as their mistrust of the establishment's ability to understand and/or identify with their sociological experience and struggles as a race within society; perpetuating the need to defend restorative justice within black communities.

Tia arrived early for her first counselling session. She thought she would be nervous. However, she was quite excited, curious about what would happen and how she would react.

"Good afternoon, Tia."
"Afternoon, Dr Collins." She studied his well-chiselled features, blue eyes and fading tan.

Her counsellor was calm and quietly spoken; she found the session quite cathartic.

Following all the general introductions, Dr Collins said, "Good to see you this morning,"

Tia laughed, "I'm not sure it's good,"

"How are you this week?"

"I am fine," Tia then felt awkward, wondering what to say next.

Dr Collins tried to put her at ease, asking questions about her week and talking about the weather outside. "What do you expect from this session?"

"I don't know, to talk about my past, to feel better about myself."

"You want to feel better about yourself?"

"Yeah, where should I start?"

He then launched into the session. "What is your earliest memory?"

"Drinking a bottle, laying on my back in the cot."

"That's way back, great. Any others?"

"A nasty smell of kidneys cooking in the kitchen. I was about five."

"OK," he sat quietly,

"My bedroom door shifting open, quietly in the middle of the night and me being scared."

"How old were you?"

"Six, maybe."

"Do you remember any more?"

Tia suddenly felt uncomfortable talking to Dr Collins, having been violated by another man. She sat with the feeling, braced herself, then continued.

"He hurt me," her eyes welled up, and she dipped her head forward.

Dr Collins sat silently for a few moments. Tia thought this lasted forever. She was afraid to go on.

"It's OK to talk about it, Tia,"
"He took away my innocence; I was a little girl. How could he do that to me?"

"What did he do Tia?"

Tia gripped her mouth. "It was our little secret,"

Dr Collins looked on attentively.

"He made me play with him, touch him in places, and he penetrated me," Tia was in floods of tears. Dr Collins leaned forward, maintaining eye contact whenever possible. She couldn't hear what Dr Collins was saying. She was hurting so badly and wanted to escape her own mind, but there was nowhere else to go.

She then sat still.

Tia then said, "I couldn't stop him, I didn't know it was wrong. By the time I knew my other friends didn't have secrets, I had joined in with his dirty little secret. He made me want to. I couldn't help feeling the feelings at the time. Later I couldn't do it anymore and hated him for trying to keep me there, trapped in his sick games." In a world of her own, staring at the carpet, Tia continued, "In the gang, I had to suck head and have sex with the *olders*. Marcel let 'em."

"Who was Marcel?"

"An older woman, she might have been in her twenties."

As the session drew to a close, Dr Collins paraphrased a lot about what had been disclosed and discussed and how she felt about it. Tia was mentally and physically exhausted, she felt as though she had been to battle. Telling someone else brought a sense of relief. Like sharing her burden without judgement.

44.

Denzil had been placed in isolation off the main ward under police guard.

Two officers entered the room, "My name is DC Polldark, and this is Officer McCarthy. We have a few questions to ask you," he continued, "The staff nurse tells us that you are on the mend."

Denzil was apprehensive. DC Polldark began drilling down, questioning him about what events had taken place.

"I don't remember anything about the assault, other than the two man who approached me in the street and asked me for my wallet. They tried to frisk me before beating me up."

"How many men were there?"

"Two, definitely."

"So, you were just walking down the street, and they approached you?"

"Yeah."

"Could you identify them if you saw them again?"

"Maybe, I don't know."

"What were you doing in an industrial estate late at night?"
"They led me there at knifepoint."

"Who were you visiting in the area?"

"A friend."

"Who?"

Denzil thought: *Why would they ask me that, do they know something I don't?* He then answered, "You don't need that information, it's not relevant. I am tired, my chest hurts,"

"OK, we will be back during the week. Thanks."

Later that afternoon, Tyresse walked in. Denzil panicked. "The feds are going on dodgy, asking me bogus questions bruv. They know something, wait... is there CCTV cameras round there?"

"Oh, what, you think they saw something?"

"Possibly, listen, we need to get our stories straight," he was mystified,

"But why the hype?"

"They asked me how many men jumped me and I told them two."

Tyresse responded saying, "There was at least five, man, dem when I came, what if they saw me going into the industrial estate before they came out? Who might they have seen going in or coming out?"

Denzil rubbed his chin in thinking mode. Tyresse sat silently, leaning forward, also with his hand on his chin.

The police picked Tyresse up on the street later that afternoon in connection with Junior's murder. They brought him into an interview room with a wooden table in the centre. DC Polldark and another officer sat in on the interview.

DC Polldark began his interrogation "There was another serious incident involving another young lad in the same vicinity last week Friday, and he described his attackers as five young men in their late teens to mid-twenties with balaclavas. Were you aware that incident had taken place and who the perpetrators might be?"

"No,"

DC Polldark shoved a photo in front of Tyresse. It was indeed a photo of him crossing the road as he entered the Industrial estate at 22:15. DC Polldark explained that six young men had entered the industrial estate 20 minutes before his arrival. "We believe one of those young people to be Denzil, their faces were covered so we couldn't get a clear view of the individuals from this shot. Tell us what you know Tyresse."

"I didn't see anyone else there."

"Come on Tyresse, do you expect us to believe that?"

"I don't know."

It was cold and damp when Tyresse left the police station. *What do they know that they are not telling me?* he thought. His phone rang out in the night - unknown number, "Who's dat?"

"De grim reaper, mind what you say to de feds, you see what happen a couple weeks back, that might be you and your friend boss."

Tyresse wrestled through the night wondering what information the police had. He thought: *What does D really know?*

Tyresse woke up late. He was distressed. *I escaped from this life:* he thought. He asked himself, "How did I get here man and how do I get out?"

Tyresse rushed through the entrance of the hospital. He was late.

"What time you call dis man?" Denzil was annoyed.

"I had things to do D. The police know you and I were on the estate with those guys. Do you know the guy they beat up a couple of weeks back?" There was a long silence. Tyresse looked round at Denzil.

"Remember Junior who lived nearby the Green?" Denzil whispered

Tyresse looked hesitant "What, little Junior?"

"Yeah."

"It's him, he owed dough too? They killed him; man told me he died in hospital this week." Tyresse took a deep breath.

"He had coke, crack, heroin, you name it, but didn't bring the dough man."

"Who killed him, D?"

"I don't know."

"Don't take the piss man, tell me."

"Serious, I don't know where my supplier buys his stuff. T, do you think that they are linking the two incidents bruv? How though?"

"They are investigating a homicide bruv. I can see where they're going with this, the pressure is probably on to find the murderers man, and you're linked D. Don't you get it?"

"But I don't know them, and you've paid the money."

"Yeah, but now the feds are after you man, and I am being implicated."

45.

Tracey sat on the edge of her bed wondering how she planned to disguise her eating habits from Tyresse. He was on to her, and she did not know how to deal with it. She wondered if her parents knew, but never said. Who knew? She was now frustrated. She felt faint and lay back on her back.

She now stood in front of the mirror. Her flesh sat like peach peel around her bones. Her waist was ultra-slender and her cheekbones prominent. She stared into the mirror for 30 minutes, studying her form.

Am I big boned? she thought. She had been using coconut mousse to thicken her hair strands. She noted something was different but couldn't put her finger on it. She doubled up in pain. She was hungry but thought about the scales in the morning. She then recalled panicking whilst staying at Tyresse's home because his mother served her what she considered to be a huge plate of food as a side dish, as she said she didn't eat a lot, then left it on the side.

She then consoled herself saying, "I ate breakfast the following morning so, I made up for dinner the previous night." She then told herself, anyway, "a minute on the lips is a lifetime on the hips." She was going over to Tyresse tonight and wondered what Brenda would cook for dinner. On the bus she began stressing out about how much she should eat, as the food kept coming; Brenda's way of making her feel welcome. She thought: *Yeah, I'll say I had dinner before I came.*

Tracey looked down at the hot steaming plate of Bolognese and pasta.

"Don't let it get cold, Tray," Brenda urged her on. Brenda and Tyresse studied Tracey across the table. "What's the matter Tracey, you haven't touched your food?"

"I'm waiting for it to cool down,"

Brenda looked concerned and shot a glance at Tyresse.

20 minutes had gone by, and Tracey was drinking water from her glass. Tyresse was now looking firmly at Tracey. Tracey looked down at her plate. She began to breathe quickly. Her hands were shaking. Brenda had a look of concern on her face. Tracey rapidly excused herself from the table and ran to the bathroom. Tyresse went up after her.

"Tray, open the door."

"Not now Ty."

"Tracey." Tyresse stood quietly outside the door while Brenda cleared the dishes away. She opened the door slowly, she had been crying. Looking at her, Tyresse realised that she had lost more weight. He blew through his lips and stared in front of him.

"Tray, what's going on?"

"I'm not eating properly, just been tired lately."

"Did you really think you were pregnant?" Tyresse focused his stare in front of him. "Tell me the truth, don't lie to me."

"I was scared Ty; I didn't know what to say." She began crying again. Tyresse stretched out his arms and embraced her. She then began to sob. They stood there for 20 minutes in silence, she just sobbed.

The silence was broken. "This can't carry on, what you going to do?"

"I don't know. See my doctor, I suppose."

Later that night, Tracey's mind raced. She thought: *They are going to make me eat. They going to try and force me to do what I don't want to do. They can't make me.* She was again very distressed.

The next day, Tracey met with Tia and Aarti. It was the weekend. She was tired and grateful not to have outstanding assignments.

"Girl, you look a mess. You look like death warmed up; what happened to you?"

"Alright Tia, don't rub it in, I had a rough night,"

"What happened?"

"Couldn't sleep, that's all, stress of coursework, deadlines, I'm up to my neck in it."

Aarti stretched out her hand and rested it on Tracey's, "You sure everything is OK? You look unwell, Tracey.   Are you eating properly?" Tracey withdrew her hand and pulled it aggressively through her hair.

"What is this, pick on Tracey day? Lay off, will you?"

"Tracey, we didn't mean to upset you, calm down."

"T, I am fine, just mind yours and get off my back, OK?" widening her eyes.

At that moment Tracey was petrified to even consider what life would be like without her regimented routines. She dared to imagine how she would cope listening to someone else's ideas about what was the right way to be. She couldn't imagine not going home and counted out 4 level tablespoons of dinner into a saucer, Then wrapped the remainder in newspaper and shoved it to the bottom of the bin so that Archie didn't notice.

Both Tia and Aarti looked on intently, wondering what was wrong.

Tia then said, "Anyway, I've decided to continue my counselling sessions 'cause it helps me to discover who I am and what I need. My identity will take time to unravel. For the first time in forever, I can say I care what I think about me. I know that I want to heal, to get better, to deal with my crap, however scary it is."

Tracey then said, "Yeah, OK, I didn't come here for a counselling session, listening to you bang on about your feelings and your identity."

"Tracey that's it, I've had enough, you're behaving like a real bitch. What's your problem? What's got into you today, spit it out; go on,"

Tia and Aarti froze, staring at Tracey. She sat still, staring down at the pencil she was knocking against the table. Tracey then rubbed her hands together and brought them down gently to rest on the table, picked up her bag and left.

"What is going on?" Aarti looked around to see where Tracey was going.
Tia responded saying, "God knows, but it ain't the bull crap she fed us."

"Anyway, how are wedding plans going for you? You haven't said a lot since you've been back."

"I need more time to think things through."

"Like what?"

"He is a lovely guy; I should count myself lucky."

"Oh no! what's wrong, why are you second guessing yourself? Listen to the quiet voice inside, OK."

Aarti smirked. "I just need more time to process things,"

"It sounds to me like the cart is going before the horse."

"What?" Aarti looked puzzled.

"Wait for you to catch up; to agree to the wedding."

"I am not opposed to the wedding; I just need time to think it through."

"Then, what are you unsure about?"

"I am thinking about my studies, my profession, seeing the world. Ajay is very traditional. He wants a home and a family. He sees himself as the provider."

"That's good, isn't it? Sounds like a plan to me, someone to look out for you."
"He wants to come to Britain, for us to make a life here."

"Isn't that what you want too?"

"Yes, I want to be happy; I just need time to think it through."

Tia raised her eyebrows and sighed. "Then take all the time you need; simple, right?"

Simple was hardly the way Aarti would describe it. Tia felt like an imposter, giving advice about something she had no knowledge of. She longed for a meaningful love relationship, where a man was keen to know her mind, not rummage through her body. There were times when she wasn't even present in body, mind or spirit. When would she trust a man's intention to love and respect her as she was? She was beginning to understand that her happiness was hers to create and for others to enjoy with her. She says in a small voice, "My saga continues." she laughed, physically patting herself on the back at the table.

46.

Xavier sat in the canteen, talking to Tia. He was somewhat distracted. Tia observed this. She sat looking at Xavier. *My prey*: she thought. Talking to herself, she said, "No! Tia see it for what it really is. You slept with him, and he took the goods. I volunteered MYSELF without thinking about whether he was actually interested in me. That's not cool, that's sad!" She then thought: *Wait a minute, why are you being so hard on yourself? At the end of the day, it's women's lib, and I can express myself. Women are not here to be dominated by men.* She then leaned forward and kissed Xavier full on the lips.

He looked up, "Wow, why did you do that?"

"Why not?" She felt powerful and smiled. Xavier smiled back.

"What you doing later?" Xavier said in a low raspy voice.

"I'm about,"

They smiled at one another. "See you later then, T,"

"Yep, around 10,"

"Great." Xavier smiled triumphantly as he walked away, saying, "Easy peasy." As he left the canteen to make his way to lectures, he telephoned Tyresse, "What you up to? I haven't heard from you."

"I'm in class."
"OK, see you in a minute."

"How's your cousin?"

"He's good."

"Still in hospital?"

"Yep."

"It's all sorted now right?"

"It's a bit messy man."

Bleep: a message on Tyresse's phone from DC Polldark: NEW LEAD, CAN YOU ATTEND THE STATION TODAY? I AM HERE UNTIL 19:30.

What do they want with me man? :he thought.

"You going in?"

"Yeah."

Tyresse stood outside the police station. *This is all too familiar*: he thought: *I don't want this. I don't plan to be cut off from the economic chain; buried in spent convictions. I don't want this.* For the first time, he truly understood the value of his liberty. The growing disparity between rich and poor. Bondman and Freeman. Tyresse stood in the rain and prayed, "Father, I need your intervention today!"

"Good evening Tyresse, I have some more questions for you." DC Polldark sounded resolute; assured of what he was saying.

"All seven young people, including yourself were on the estate for at least 15 to 20 minutes before five people left. Did you all agree to meet up? If so what did you discuss? Was there an exchange of drugs or money?" He continued the barrage of questioning, "We know you frequent the Millharbour housing estate."

"My cousin lives there."

"We're dealing with a homicide which took place there a fortnight ago. We know your cousin was assaulted elsewhere and brought to the industrial estate and that you were the first on the scene."

"He called my phone."

"You entered the industrial estate with a small paper bag in your hand and left empty-handed. Money, or drugs perhaps?"

Tyresse sat still with his arms crossed.

"Where did your cousin tell you he was when he rang?"

"I don't know."

"Paramedics stated that Denzil was virtually unconscious when they arrived, so was not in any fit state to make that call." Polldark pressed on, "What time did he call?"

"I don't remember."

"You're not likely to remember because he never called you from his phone."

"What?" Tyresse exclaimed, "I am sure it was his voice!"
Polldark straightened himself and folded his arms. Tyresse focused on the stain splash on the wall.

Tyresse then said, "Are you going to arrest me? Otherwise, I want to leave; I have nothing else to say."

"Can I check the number that called you?" DC Polldark was leaning over Tyresse.

"It was a no-caller ID."

"I see; can I check the time of the call?" DC Polldark noted the time in his notebook. "You can go for now."

Tyresse left the trenches and headed for the front doors. He took a deep breath and headed home.

47.

DC Polldark strolled through the ward, hoping to advance in the homicide investigation. He entered the room. Denzil sat up straight.

He had spoken to Tyresse that morning on the basher phone.

"Good morning, Denzil. We spoke to Tyresse last night about some anomalies relating to your rescue, and the sums don't add up."

Denzil watched as DC Polldark sauntered around the bed. *He's trying to intimidate me*: he thought.

"Did you make a phone call to Tyresse the night he found you?"

"I don't remember; it was all a blur."

"That's interesting, how then did he know where to find you?"

"I don't know."

Polldark pulled out a photograph. Denzil froze; it was a photograph of Junior. "Do you recognise him? This photo was taken the night before he was assaulted and battered."

"Yeah,"

"A friend?"

"He lived on the estate."

DC Polldark paused, "Do you have the same friends?"

"He might have known people I know, I didn't know," Denzil scratched his head.

"We saw a message on his WhatsApp from a person signed D, could that be you?"

"No, I don't know him like dat," Denzil flexed his nostrils but sat perfectly still with his arms crossed. DC Polldark, stood to face him, noting the defensive stance taken.

"What's your telephone number? It would help our investigation."

Denzil volunteered a number, any number. "That will be it for now. Goodbye, Denzil."

Tyresse was early. Nevertheless, he was allowed to go in. Tyresse muscled in close and whispered to Denzil, "They know the time those boys called, but the number's not traceable. Listen D, T dot threatened to deal with me if I say anything that will incriminate them."

"The police asked me my number, I gave them any number innit, I'm not worried, I was using a basher. I don't even know what those boys did with the phone, cha, that was one of my lines, man."

"They probably took it over."

"Yeah. Ty, they're trying to link us to Junior's murder."

"What, that's nuts. Last night they asked me about the money I had in my pocket. They saw it on CCTV and me leaving with my hands empty."

"Listen, Ty, tell them…"

Tyresse interjected, "I will know what to say, man. I never saw anyone, but you in the industrial park and they can't prove any different."

Officer McCarthy appeared in the doorway. "Just the two young people I wanted to see." Both Denzil and Tyresse fixed their eyes on him. Officer McCarthy strolled up to Denzil and placed a photo on the bed alongside him. It was a photo of him and Junior walking down the High street together with another young person. PC McCarthy explained this was several days before Junior was assaulted. Tyresse never took his eyes away from the photo, and McCarthy was observant of their reactions.

"I said I knew him on the estate but it's not like that, he's not one of my peoples innit," Denzil was defiant.

"We have information stating otherwise Denzil."

"Listen, I had nothing to do with dat."

"With what Denzil?" Officer McCarthy was looking at him inquisitively.

"What, you think I killed him bruv? Nah, don't pin dat on me bruv."

"Chill out D," Tyresse stood in his face.

PC McCarthy then said, "We've been told you both pushed drugs on the streets. Did he owe money? Upset the wrong punter? Better to admit it now than be caught out."

Tyresse then noticed the officer stationed outside the room, inside the corner of the room.

"I don't know what you're on about, I don't know nothing." Denzil threw his hands into the bedding.
"We will keep digging Denzil, it's just a matter of time."

Both officers left the room.

"Don't worry man, they're just trying to work your brain bruv, hold it down," said Tyresse in a reassuring tone. Denzil felt tired and complained of pains in his head. There was still a lot of swelling around the eye and cheek area on the left side where he had repeatedly been punched. "I'll let you rest man, come and see you tomorrow."

"OK, bro." Denzil looked out of the window and thought: *I can't tell Tyresse the whole story.*

Junior and Denzil bought a 'Z' of snow, sold all of it and made a profit. They considered themselves in business and bought more drugs including, crack and heroin. The second time around, they supported their lavish lifestyle. Easy come easy go, not calculating monies owed for goods purchased. The deadlines for payment were extended, then D-day arrived. The grim reaper came to collect, and the debt had been paid, in part, with Junior's life. Denzil was now distraught and riddled with guilt. He thought: *He wasn't supposed to die. They pushed it too far man, and now the feds are trying to push it on me.*

Tyresse felt sorry for Denzel, bruised and busted, scared and confused. Tyresse thought: *He's defenceless.* Denzil lay still staring through the hospital blinds in his room, hoping to catch a glimpse of life outside in the hallway.

Denzil spoke out, "Ty, trusts me man, but man gotta eat out here. I feel a way but." Denzil kisses his teeth. "I need to pull my weight, hold down tings, be my own man." Denzil's heart was heavy. Being a man was more important than being loyal to his cousin. *No value in that:* he thought: *couldn't earn any pees. What good is loyalty when you can't eat?* He then tried to convince himself of a lie. "Man isn't thinking of me bruv." However, he couldn't extinguish or deny the love and blood ties between them. "You know what," flinging his arms in the air. "What he doesn't know won't hurt him."

His conscience battled on.

48.

Xavier's chest descended. He lay stretched out on the floor in the living room. He was used to his own company, contemplating his next move, his life's ambitions and conquests. "I need stimulation," he uttered out loud. "Those tutors are mediocre; they should be done trying to convince us students of time-warped ideals. What do I really want?" he thought to himself: *I want silence from the noise of life's dreary and arduous nature.* He needed some water to wash down the pill he had just taken.

"You got an opener?" Tyresse called out from the kitchen.

"Yep, in the bottom draw cabinet."

"Yeah, I see it." Tyresse sat down, near Xavier.

"What's happening with Denzil?"

"The feds are trying to pin a murder on him. We kinda knew him at school but not like close friends or anything."

"Damn, I wouldn't wish that on my worst enemy, and he's busted."

"Bad news at the moment man."

"I'm wasted," Xavier leaned forward.

"You what, why?" Tyresse began to laugh. Xavier began singing out loud, and Tyresse laughed even louder.

"I am looking in the mirror," stretching his arms out, "And I see a Titan. A masterpiece," Tyresse looked over at him. "I am invincible, all-powerful," Xavier was now standing up and waving to the crowds, looking all around him. Tyresse sat back, wondering what was happening. Xavier kneeled alongside Tyresse and said, "We live underground, in the crust of the flat earth; shush," placing his index finger over his lips.

Tyresse smiled, "You're buzzing, man. What have you taken? Go to bed and sleep it off." Tyresse lit a spliff and sat quietly until Xavier calmed down.

After a couple of hours or so, Xavier looked across at Tyresse and said, "Ah man, how long you been here?"

"A few hours."

"Where did I go this time?"

"Middle-earth." They looked at each other and roared with laughter.

"The girls love you, don't they?"

Tyresse looked at Xavier, "Course man, I am all that, you know it."

"You're shit confident, I love that."

"You got to love you, man," Tyresse was beating on his chest. Xavier admired his charisma.

Tyresse began to boast, "The girls call me blow torch," Tyresse started laughing to himself,

"They don't call me anything," Xavier smirked at himself. He looked solemn and felt sad.

"Let me teach you some moves," Tyresse was in his element and had not noticed that Xavier was downcast.

Xavier, you are pathetic: a woman's voice invaded his head, crystal clear, close to his earlobe. His eyes darted to the front door. "Who's that?" he shouted.

"Who's what?" Tyresse sprang to attention. "You OK, man?"

"She's wrong, I am a god."

"Xavier, you're switching. Hey," Tyresse called out in an effort to distract him.

"No! No!" Xavier gripped his upper torso and shook his head violently.

Tyresse was now on his feet and alert. "Xavier, look at me, look at me," Xavier was looking around the room and through the kitchen.

"I'm OK," Xavier exhaled.

"I was shook," Tyresse approached him.

"That was a high man," Xavier laughed, "I'm still coming down that's all. Let's go for a drink."

"I'm not carrying you home, Xavier. Rest up for tonight, and I'll see you tomorrow, don't be late."

Truthingdom

Xavier made himself a coffee and sat in the lounge alone. He was used to the solitude. The silence caressed him but stalked him at the same time.

Even amongst others, I'm solo: he thought. He felt heavy and miserable. *I feel like crap:* he thought. He imagined a dominatrix standing on his chest with stiletto heels on. He could feel her heels burrowing into his rib cage. He was then staring into the beautiful eyes of the frozen sparrow. Then everything went blank.

49.

Aarti was staring out of the window in her bedroom. She was thinking about Ajay and the conundrum regarding *the wedding*. Family reputation, above all else. She grappled with herself, knowing the importance of family pride, the family name. She knew that shame would bear irreparable consequences to the very existence, the cultural integrity, as well as the socio-economic wellbeing of the extended family.

What pressures are brought to bear? She felt crushed under the bureaucracy of broader family and local community politics. She understood that tradition takes the lead and she graciously followed. Should she be the bearer of bad karma? Does he deserve a doubting bride? Can he claim to be blissfully ignorant of free will in this age?

She conceded; was she convincing herself that she had a choice? And was that right? According to who? She clawed her way out of the imaginary swamp and went into the kitchen. A video call came through. It was Ajay.

"Hi, how are you?"

"I am well Aarti, how are you doing?"

"I am OK."

"How are the wedding plans going with your auntie?"

Truthingdom

"OK, I saw her last week."

"Your hair looks nice."

"Thank you, I haven't done anything different," stroking the back of her hair.

"How are your studies going?"

"Very well actually."

"Good, good."

"Your parents, are they OK?"

"Yes fine. I saw your parents last weekend; we went for dinner."

"I know, Mum told me."

"It's been eight days since we last spoke."

"I get so busy here with coursework and everything."

"Everything?"

"Adjusting to a new city, wedding plans, you know."

"OK, yes, great."

"How is work?"

"Fine, I am thinking about possibilities in London, quite exciting,"

"OK."

"Aarti, I miss you."

"That's so sweet."

"I think of you all the time."

"Ajay," she smiled.
He laughed, "I am so happy."

"The holidays will come around soon, and I will be visiting again."

"I can't wait."

"We can speak again this week, hopefully."

"Yes, I will call you."

"OK, bye for now."

"Goodbye Aarti, sweet dreams."

She sat in silence and purposefully blanked out her mind. However, her heart weighed heavily on her conscience.

Aarti's mind rested on Tracey. *What was wrong?* :she wondered. She was worried and distracted over the weekend. She had never seen Tracey that agitated before. Aarti thought she looked tired and thin. Perhaps she needs to rest, coursework getting on top of her. Unlike me, Tracey has a life. I just have my studies to focus on. Oh, she thought, the wedding also.

Aarti was mindful that she sat squarely on the fence and had not made any definitive decisions about whether to wed or not.

She decided to call Tracey.
"Hello Tracey, how are you?"

"Good."

"You feeling better?"

"Yeah."

"Great."

"Let's not talk about me, how are things with you? You don't talk about," she paused, "what happened?"

There was a long pause.

"I don't think about it; it was very traumatic you know."

"Yeah," Tracey said softly.

"I feel a pain in my heart, I cannot tell my family."

"Why? Why Aarti? You're the victim here, you were violated."

"It would be frowned upon; getting married, I cannot talk of such things. Across the border near my country, they stone women for such things. Men take virgins who are not married, it goes unpunished."

"So, what are you telling me? You are just going to leave it?"

"What can I do Tracey?"

"Can you remember what colour he was, big man, small man, short, tall?" Tracey cross-examined Aarti.

"Tall, white or darker skin; It was dark, I don't remember."

"OK."

"Actually, he had a tattoo on his thigh. I told the police about this."

"Right, any leads so far?"

"Not that I am aware of, I have a lot on my mind."

"Yeah, I know. Are you bitter?"

"Not really, in my country wives are treated worse."

"Are you saying you forgive him?"

"Yes, otherwise I am my own jailer."

Tracey then said, "I watched my dad beat and take advantage of my Mum and could not do anything to defend her. Aarti, I watched, when I closed my eyes I heard the blows, the screams, there was no escape. I remember wetting myself once because I was so traumatised." Tracey began to cry.

"Tracey, I am listening to you, and I hear your pain."

Truthingdom

"I am so over it, all of them."

"What do you mean?"

"I suffered so much and loved at the same time, it's twisted, they hate me now." She was sobbing.

"Why do they hate you?"

"Because I am with Tyresse," she now sounded defiant.

"You need to do what is right in your heart. Love is stronger than hate Tracey," she paused, "give it time."

"All these years I've suffered; then they reject me at the drop of a hat."

"Drop of a hat?"

"Oh, it's a saying. They abandoned me just like that."

"They don't know, they don't understand, give them time."

"Am I not paying you, girl? Whose side are you on?"

"The side of mercy. Please be patient, all will be well,"

"Huh, you don't know my lot."

"Does Tyresse make you happy, does he respect you and treat you well?"

"Yeah, he does."

"Well then, just take time OK?"

"Thanks Aarti, good night."

Aarti reflected on the advice she had given Tracey. She spoke freely about love and the right to love who you want to love. Was that how she really felt? She pondered, does love conquer all? Above family and honour. Was she being a hypocrite, telling Tracey one thing and believing another. Who was right the eastern or western concept, to love freely or not. she thought: *I am in London now, why not love freely? Are the English not civilised, to say they can love without conditions?* She dared to think in a way other than she had ever known.

I am here to learn new things, meet new people. What if I choose to embrace and adopt new ways? She gripped her elbows with both hands around her diaphragm and blew out through the restricted hole between her lips.

Would she ever be forgiven for loving without her parent's consent? Would she be prepared to gamble and possibly lose? She grabbed the empty brown paper bag on the cabinet and blew into it. Aarti was now staring into the mirror. Her face appeared blank; without expression: *What will I do? Whose needs will I serve? Mine, my parents or Ajay's?*

Interlude

Are you looking in the mirror, who do you really see!
Who's staring back at you? Do you recognise the person?

Tia *battles repetition and low self-esteem, will she battle and win against forces who denounce her right to be strong; to be tenacious of mind.*

Xavier *dreams above the clouds, missing the ignoble below. Those without significance, he scoffs at.*

Tyresse, *dark chocolate; described as exotic; unwittingly dabbles in the dark recesses of Denzil's mind; unguarded.*

Tracey, *amber delight, sits in the mercy seat, enslaved by her own trappings, starved of self- compassion.*

Aarti, *attempting to fly with clipped wings, unsure of her destination, her destiny her desires.*

All five are battling their nemesis whilst journeying inward, deeper into their own ego's and their misguided truths.

Can your judgement and ideals of the scenario's presented before you, set them free from their own inhibitions and yours?

Look straight ahead and decipher what your conscience knows. What your heart feels and desires.

Welcome to the ongoing journey, moving forward into the infinite in book two: **Truthingdom: The Revelation.**

Omnificent!

Contact Roslyn Blaize

 Blaizetheauthor@gmail.com

 Blaizetheathor

Publishers Afterword

Rose
Congratulations on the relaunch!

To success!

Marcia M Spence

Marcia M Publishing House

www.marciampublishing.com

23871798R00128

Made in the USA
Columbia, SC
18 August 2018